In the Appalachian Ohio River town of East Liverpool, people struggle to make and remake their lives. Old and young, they find success and loss in mythic imagination and everydayness. Karen Kotrba's interwoven short stories share human aspirations and actions with insight, humor, and compassion.

These citizens of *Pottery Town*, which someone wryly names "Poverty Town", make full accountings of themselves through observation and interactions at a parade, in homes, apartments, streets, stores, and cafés. Each story bubbles with history and place, sight, sound, and taste. Each creates a cinematic, richly detailed scene. The author leads us along store aisles, blind alleys, and misdirections to unexpected, yet satisfying conclusions. Henry David Thoreau's adage, found printed on a small pack of sugar, may say it best: "There is no remedy for love but to love more." Kotrba treats us to this.

—Kathleen S. Burgess, author of
What Burden Do Those Trains Bear Away: A Memoir in Poems

OTHER BOOKS BY KAREN KOTRBA

*She Who is Like a Mare: Poems of Mary Breckinridge
and the Frontier Nursing Service* (Bottom Dog Press, 2012)

BOTTOM DOG PRESS

HURON, OHIO

POTTERY TOWN BLUES

KAREN KOTRBA

APPALACHIAN WRITING SERIES
BOTTOM DOG PRESS
HURON, OHIO

Bottom Dog Press, Inc.
PO Box 425, Huron, OH 44839
Lsmithdog@aol.com
http://smithdocs.net

CREDITS:
General Editor: Susanna Sharp-Schwacke
Cover & Layout Design: Susanna Sharp-Schwacke
Cover Art: Sheri Liebschner, "East Liverpool, Ohio Cityscape,
View from the Ohio River." www.sheriliebschner.com

ACKNOWLEDGMENTS:
The author wishes to thank the Northeast Ohio MFA pro-
gram and the Ohio Arts Council.
"Death Mask" first appeared in *Whiskey Island*, "And Your
Name Is?" in *Adanna Literary Journal*, and "First Stone" in *Penguin Review*.
"Death Mask: was first read in 2019 at the Writers Association of
Northern Appalachia Conference
"The Remedy for Love" was read in 2018 at the Youngstown
Lit's Literary Festival in 2018.

TABLE OF CONTENTS

For those who sustain me:
Annie Gaffney, Lonnis Krisher, Jan C. Snow,
Patti Swartz, and the memory of Agnes Frank.

What are we up against, those of us who aspire to become inhabitants, who wish to commit ourselves to a place?

—Scott Russell Sanders, *Staying Put*

DEATH MASK

Most times I can coax Pretty into the car, but he will not wear a seatbelt and the only place he'll get out at is the bank.

"Watch," I told him the first time we went. "This is how *I* make a withdrawal." He laughed. Up to then he'd rarely so much as smiled. He'd been at my place a of couple weeks at that point, mostly looking out the window, scowling. But it was sunny the day we went to the bank, and that must have made a difference. Whatever it was, he looked a lot better than the sad man who'd followed me home from the Lots & Lots.

"You're a good woman, Aggie," he said when he stopped laughing. And right then I knew we'd be all right.

A couple of days before that we were in the kitchen. Pretty sat at the table while I made dinner: breaded pork chops with sauerkraut and noodles and applesauce and green beans. I wouldn't make all that fuss if it was just me. Anyway, Pretty seemed real sad, and I told him, "I seen you before, you know. Not you in person, but your face."

"A picture?" He turned to me. "I was in all the papers."

No, it wasn't a picture. See, after Pretty died Daddy took me to the police station where the death mask was on display. Pretty Boy Floyd's death was big news around here 'cause he was such a famous bank robber. Word got around fast, farmers left their fields and folks came from across the river just to see Pretty's mask. J. Edgar Hoover had named him Public Enemy Number One, and people wanted to see his body for themselves, though by then it was on a train headed back to Oklahoma. But the undertaker had

11

made a death mask, so people were excited to hear that there was something to look at after all.

Daddy said we were at the hardware store, him and me, when someone told about the mask. The store was crowded and busy. Oh, nearly every place in East Liverpool was bustling back then. All the potteries were running, making dishes that were sold all over the country. East Liverpool used to be called the Tabletop Capital of America, and I can believe it. Most people had a job— in the potteries or the mills mostly—and they were earning good money, so the stores were always busy with people buying things.

Anyway, on this particular day, when people in the hardware store heard about the death mask they set down what they were looking at and left. It never occurred to Daddy to take me home, so there I was, holding his hand when we walked into the police station and a crowd of noisy men. One man was saying what a hardened criminal Pretty was, worse than all those other gangsters put together, and others were nodding and saying, "Yes, sir. That's right."

When Daddy held me up to see the mask, I reached out as if I wanted to touch it, so he worked his way through the crowd and held me close to it. And just like that, I stretched out my little arm—oh, I wasn't much more than a toddler back then—and I did touch that face. It was smooth and cool, and I said, "Daddy, why did they shoot this handsome man?"

Well, Daddy always said that after that a man started talking about what a dirty shame it was the G-men shot Pretty down like that, all of them against just one fellow and him already caught with nowhere left to run. And another man said, "That Purvis fellow never gave Pretty a chance to give up. That's what I heard." The whole crowd changed its mind in just that moment, Daddy said. And all because a little child had shamed them.

Now, how I met Pretty was like this. Easter was coming, and I had just come out of the Lots & Lots with a cart full of plastic eggs and inflatable bunnies. The neighborhood Easter egg hunt was going to be on Saturday, and it's always held in my yard because I'm the only one without dogs. I had intended to just buy plastic eggs and a whole lot of candy, but when I got in there, I saw these giant blow-up bunnies. They must have been six feet tall, and the price was so good I bought four, one in each color. Plus, it was a Tuesday when seniors get another ten percent off their total purchase. We got a lot of babies on our street right now, and I thought they'd get a real kick out of those bunnies.

It was cold that day I went shopping, and the clouds were big and low. It was about two o'clock and almost dark already. Looked like night was gonna slam down hard any minute. The slush in the parking lot was trying to freeze again, and it was hard work pushing the cart. I was concentrating so hard that I almost ran into a man who was standing in front of me. He wore a slouch hat and a suit with lapels wider than those old ones at the Goodwill.

"'Scuse me," I said, but he didn't look up. I went to my car and popped the trunk. For some reason, I turned around and seen he was still there.

"Forget where you parked?" I asked.

Nothing. He kept looking at the ground and took a step or two away from me.

"Did you drop something?"

Nothing again. Still staring down at the ground, still walking real slow.

"Did you drop your keys in the snow?"

He stopped then and looked right at me but only for a second. Still, he didn't say a word. He just walked away.

All right for some, I thought, and I left. But it troubled me. At first I thought he was rude not to speak, but he looked so forlorn. And that hat. Men don't wear hats anymore. They wear these ball caps that make them look like big children, but not proper hats. Every time Daddy went into town, he would put on his fedora— just to show them he meant business.

The next day I was going somewhere when I turned into the Lots & Lots without giving it a thought, and right away I saw

13

him, doing it all again, walking all over the lot with his head down. A few years before when my sister Cissy tried wearing contact lens, she'd no sooner get them in than one would pop out and she'd shout, "Don't move!" Me and Rose Anne would have to stand frozen while Cissy searched all over the floor. The man in the slouch hat reminded me of that. I parked my car and walked up to him.

"Honey," I said. "Can I help you find whatever it is you're looking for?" He smiled. I hadn't expected a smile, but that's what he did, and I could see he had these huge Clark Gable dimples. He put his hand up to his hat, the way men used to do when they were acting like they just might tip it to you.

"Well, ma'am," he said. "I appreciate it, but I'm just looking for the way out. And I'm beginning to think there isn't one anywhere around here."

The way out? What was he talking about?

"You looking for the way in, honey? The door's up there," and I pointed to the store.

He looked where I pointed, shading his eyes with one hand as if this was a sunny day which it wasn't.

"No, that's not it, ma'am. You know anything about tunnels?"

"Mister, look around you. This has all been paved over for years. Before that, it was fields and farms. Oh, there was a mine. Used to be a coal tipple right over there. But that was a long time ago."

The man looked around, his dark eyes sharp, taking it all in, like he had made up his mind to see the fields and coal tipple that weren't there anymore. And then it came to me, and I understood.

"There's an historic marker not far from here," I said. "Even if there's almost no one left to remember what happened, this is still an important place."

He raised his head then and looked at me. His eyes were sad.

I narrowed my eyes at him. "Charles? Charles Arthur Floyd? Is that you?"

"Well, I'm not so sure as I should say," he smiled, showing off those dimples. "Lest the wrong people get wind of it, you know?"

"You've been looking for a long time," I said, and the sadness that had been in his eyes spread to the rest of his face.

"Yes, ma'am, I have. I thought, see, somebody told me there was a—""

"That was a long time ago, Charles. But you know that, don't you?"

"Yes, ma'am." His sadness went even deeper then. What could I do? Somebody had to tell him.

And then I heard myself say, "Charles, you look like you could use a sandwich. And I can't stand to think of you out here alone, just rooting around. Why don't you come home with me, and we'll sit down and figure this out? My name's Agnes, by the way. But you can call me Aggie."

"That's kind of you, ma'am." He took off his hat and twisted it in his hands.

And that's how it was. Pretty got into the car, and I drove us home. I made us both a chicken salad sandwich on a croissant and put on some coffee, and we sat down together at my kitchen table, the coffee smell moving all around us like a friendly cloud.

He's been with me ever since, and the truth is I'm happy for the company. I've been alone since Cissy died just before Christmas. She didn't talk much though, and Pretty and me talk a lot, about the weather and what's on the television. Pretty likes all the cop shows but he gets a particular kick out of that Lenny Brisco on *Law and Order*.

There are things Pretty will *not* talk about though, like what happened to him. This one time though, something he saw on one of those cop shows got him started and he said that when the G-men were hot on his trail, he hoped he could disappear, vanish like a magician, and not pop up again until he was somewhere in Pennsylvania. But he got hungry while he was on the run and stopped at a farm and asked for lunch. The farmer's wife made him a sandwich—a BLT with tomatoes from her own garden. She'd just poured Pretty a glass of milk when her husband rushed in and said, "Honey, you should see the cars and all these fellows up and down the road. Sure is something going on."

15

But when the woman turned to introduce her husband to the stranger, he was gone. Pretty didn't get far though. The G-men were closer than he thought, and while he was running across a field, they shot him. Then they carried him to a tree and set him up against the trunk. He died there, propped up against that tree. Of course, it's long gone now, and the field. And all those people too, I guess.

Cissy died this last winter, right before Christmas. At first I didn't know what to do. I was 82 years old and I had never lived alone in my life. I went straight from Momma and Daddy's house to live with my husband. He's been gone for years. Not dead gone, just left gone. When Cissy heard, she quit her job and moved in with Rose Anne and me and stayed, even after Rose Anne went off to college and got a job in Pittsburgh. Just before Christmas, Cissy's heart gave out. Sudden, in her sleep. Rose Anne started telling me all the reasons I should move to Pittsburgh. "No," I told her. "I have lived my whole life right here, and I have things to do right here, like the Easter egg hunt. I intend to stay."

Oh, and we did have an Easter egg hunt! The day was cold but sunny. It was a fooler day, the kind when the sun feels good on your face, but you're a fool if you take off your coat. The sunshine made all the colors extra bright and the big bunnies swayed a little in the breeze. There were a lot of children there, and they were all laughing and running until Margaret's little girl—Margaret lives next door—her little girl opened up one of the plastic eggs but instead of candy, there was the head of a Barbie doll. Just the head. Can you imagine? Well, it scared her so bad she cried, and there was a ruckus about who would do such a thing that never did get figured out. I have my theories.

Once that settled down, we went on with the games that we have every year. While the children were having the race where they push eggs with their noses, I happened to look up and saw Pretty standing at my living room window. Just then the sun shifted and his face looked like his death mask, pale and cold, just floating there. I was sad to see it, but then I remembered: Pretty is never

16

going to get sick, and he is never going to die. And then, the light changed again, and there was Pretty as I know him now, smiling right at me.

I almost waved.

It's sunny today too. Winter is still trying to hold on, but the snow's melting. As soon as Pretty and me stepped outside we could hear the water moving down the gutters and rushing through the creek.

"We're going to the bank today," I tell Petty, but I want to stop at the cemetery first. I got some silk flowers at the Lots & Lots to put on Cissy's grave, and Momma and Daddy's too. The silk doesn't last long, but come Memorial Day I'll put down baskets of geraniums, living things. I drive us through the cemetery gate, past that first little road and then turn left at the second. After that I only have to look for the pink marble urn that says "Vollnagle." Nobody I know. That urn must be six feet tall. Our plots are right next to it. In the glove compartment I keep a map I drew in case I forget the way. Today though—easy as always—I drive right there.

"No need for the map yet," I tell Pretty, who nods.

Still, I'm surprised when he gets out of the car and walks with me, up the little slope, to the graves.

Up to Speed

Laura Willow's coffee had gone cold. At first, she'd sipped it, noting the satisfying richness of the brew, allowing the warmth of the cup to comfort her hand, but when the conversation turned to her financial status and her future, she had put the china teacup down. Although she'd known Fred Knight as a neighbor for twenty years, she had never before consulted him as an attorney, so she was unfamiliar with his office, a surprisingly well-furnished suite above the Anytime Café in downtown East Liverpool. Her husband Dan—her late husband, she reminded herself with a pang—had, throughout their long marriage, handled all their financial matters. From the monthly bills to the annual taxes, Dan had dealt with it, organizing it all in the massive roll top desk that had been his father's. A week ago, she'd scooped all the documents into a box and delivered them to Fred. Now, as he gestured to each as he spoke, she was aware that fear was creeping from her chest to her face.

A normally buoyant man in his fifties, Fred lived with a golden retriever named Otto in the brick ranch next door to Laura. He slid a ledger across his sleek desk, pointed to the final entry, and frowned.

"I don't understand," Laura said. "What could have happened?" She tugged at the hem of her denim skirt, an old habit. She was a tall, grey-haired woman forever bothered by clothing that never seemed to fit her properly.

Fred raised eyes as woeful as Otto's whenever Laura scolded him for digging in her yard.

18

"Laura, Dan was a good man, a fine man, but he just didn't…. The business…. Well, I know I don't have to tell you that closing it took a lot out of him." Fred gestured to the ledger. "From what I see here, it looks like he made some rather poor investments and then took out equity loans on the house. He probably didn't want you to worry. I just wish he'd come to me for advice, that's all. I'm not a financial advisor, but I am a friend and…."

If only, thought Laura. *If only he'd told me. Could I have done any worse,* she wondered, and immediately felt guilty. *Maybe he thought he could turn it around on his own. Maybe he thought there was still time.*

"Thank goodness you have the insurance and IRAs," Fred added. "If you'd like me to look those over, I'd be happy to. You shouldn't have to worry about money at a time like this."

No, but I do. I do have to worry, Laura thought. The life insurance wasn't near what she thought. And the IRAs? Well, Dan, her husband of nearly forty years and her only love, had cashed those in some time ago. She'd discovered that herself when she'd unrolled the desktop a couple of days after the funeral.

And then a cold heavy thought came to her, a lightning bolt of panic: *Will I lose the house?*

Where had the money gone? They'd had no exotic vacations, no major home repairs. They did not, as the younger generation used to say, live large. Was there some awful secret in Dan's life, like a mistress who did, in fact, like to live large? It seemed unlikely. Try as she might, Laura could not imagine a secret gambling addiction, or a child from an early indiscretion that needed to be raised, or anything of the sort. But what had happened? Where could the money have gone?

Perhaps there had always been less than Laura thought.

It wasn't just Dan's decisions that had landed her in this mess, Laura knew. She had been complacent. And that complacency, she realized now, was a form of complicity. They had agreed early in their marriage that he'd manage the dry-cleaning store while she stayed home with the boys. But they hadn't revisited that decision when their two sons were grown and out on their own.

They'd continued as before with Dan running the business and "seeing to" the exterior of the house and the finances while Laura took care of the daily running of their home, served on the library board, and began a new hobby collecting doll houses.

She'd been content all those years, satisfied with what they had and happy to assume that since Dan wasn't telling her there were any problems, then surely there weren't any. Now she didn't know who she was angrier with: Dan, sweet Dan, or with herself for being too self-absorbed—too afraid—to ask questions.

And now what?

After the boys were gone, and years before Dan's heart condition had been detected and their lives changed, Laura had gotten into the habit of driving to the Pittsburgh Zoo on the occasional Wednesday morning. She would buy a cup of weak coffee and sit on a bench in front of the giraffe pen. And there she'd sit for an hour or so, sipping coffee, and marveling at the giraffes' oddly elegant walk, the delicate lift of their heads, and their improbably long, purple tongues. She'd watch as they tugged at leaves, then slowly, slowly chewed them. These acts of grace never failed to calm her.

On the Wednesday morning three weeks after her visit to Fred's office, however, Laura was wired for sound and moving fast. There was a tiny microphone at her mouth, a miniature speaker in her ear. She wore her striped shirt and polyester pants with dignity, she liked to think, remembering to keep her back straight. Somewhere Laura had read that you can look ten pounds lighter if you just stand properly.

"Welcome to Burger Meister. How may I help you?" she said over and over into the microphone. For her first few days on the job, she'd been grateful simply to be hired. She'd worried that she was unemployable, but she surprised herself when she pulled into the fast-food restaurant up the hill in Calcutta, intending to get a cup of coffee. On impulse, she'd asked for two creams and a job.

The individual tasks were easy, she discovered, a simple matter of following a series of steps over and over. But on the morning shift, speed was the primary concern. Laura noticed that she wasn't as fast as her fellow employees, or "crew members" as the manager called them. She'd been working the drive-thru window and couldn't get accustomed to talking to people who, for the first part of the transaction, she couldn't see. Out of habit, she smiled anyway, sometimes tugging on her ear lobe as she did so, another nervous habit of hers.

When they pulled up to her window, customers handed her money and then, as quickly as she could, Laura passed back the change, coffee, and bag with the egg and sausage sandwich. Almost all of her customers were alone, she noticed. And in a hurry. Most were on their way to work, she imagined.

On busy mornings Laura apologized a lot.

"I'm sorry, but your order will take a few minutes. Would you please pull over into the parking spot directly to your left? One of our servers will bring your order out just as soon as it's ready. Now, is there anything else I can do to help you?"

The last part, the question, wasn't in the script that Ben Carson, the manager, gave her. She liked to add it because it seemed natural to ask if she could be of any other assistance. The slogan of the restaurant was, after all, *Burger Meister—Where You're the Meister!*

Customers responded to her question in various ways.

Surly: "You could hurry the hell up. That would do for a start."

Long-suffering: "Look lady, my mother's in the hospital having an operation and short of getting me out of here soon with my only chance for a meal today, there is nothing you or anyone else can do."

Jocular, self-deprecating: "Hey, could you make all that northbound traffic on Route 11 disappear so I can make it to work on time for once?"

A few were gracious: "No, nothing else. But thanks."

No matter the nature of the customer's response, Laura always added a little something. "Well, that's very nice of you to

21

say so. Thank you very much and you have a great day, okay?" Or "I'm so sorry to hear about your mother, and I just wish there was something I could do to help. Now you be careful with this coffee. It's very hot, but I know that when you're in a stressful situation it's easy to be distracted and well, I just wouldn't want you to hurt yourself."

Laura had been hired a week after the manager received a corporate memo stressing the immediate need to hire older workers. A recent PBS documentary had reported on some fast-food companies' penchant for exploiting their teenage employees, and Burger Meister's CEO had, in an unfortunate moment of candor, commented on camera about "the Susie sixteen-year-olds who, thank God, couldn't care less about benefits and are the backbone of our labor force." Unfortunately, footage shot at an Illinois Burger Meister restaurant showed teen workers who looked so dispirited they could probably use some health care at that very moment. The day after the broadcast, all Burger Meister managers were instructed to hire visibly older workers as quickly as possible. Senior hires would receive the highest preference and managers who complied would receive a cash incentive. The seniors would work without benefits too, the thinking went—they had Medicare, right?—but images of their faces would disprove the documentary's claim of teen exploitation and age discrimination.

What was missing from the corporate email was the CEO's frustration. Early in his career he'd dreamt of being an innovator, but he'd been a follower instead, offering sandwich wraps and fancy coffees just because the other chains did. Under his leadership, Burger Meister was always scrambling to keep up with the competition but forever remained a step or two behind.

Laura's soon-to-be-manager took one look at her and knew she was exactly the kind of senior worker the memo was instructing him to hire, and he wanted no part of her. Ben was not a supporter of the new hiring program. Only twenty-three, he'd been the manager of store 437 for six months and he'd already encountered more than enough senior workers. He had hired them all on his own, thank you very much, long before any memos came his way heralding this as a bright new idea. But he'd found that seniors had a way of taking control, even in the job interview, and of teasing him about his age. "You're much younger than my doctors," one said, "and they are all 12." Several claimed to own shoes or tee shirts older than he. At such moments he felt more like "Kit," as his friends at community college had called him, and not "Benjamin J. Carson," the man, the manager, as his business cards declared.

Nevertheless, Ben hired Laura. She wouldn't last, he figured. She was older than his mother and she certainly looked too slow for Burger Meister's frenetic pace. And she was tall, awfully tall, taller than him and didn't tall people get bad backs or something? By her third day he figured she'd mention that her feet hurt and sometime during the second week, if she endured that long, she'd call in sick and never return. The email had not mentioned anything about retaining these new (old) employees, and there was that cash incentive to consider. He hired Laura and told her she was on a three-week probationary status.

At the start, Ben put Laura on the late-night shift. On her third night, a Saturday, Ben dropped by for a spot check just before closing and found four men of various ages and stages of inebriation huddled over cups of coffee. Placidly cruising the dining area, which should have been cleaned and closed thirty minutes earlier, was Laura with a pot of coffee and a beatific smile. It took Ben twenty minutes to clear the men out and restore order. Two of them argued vehemently all the way out the door about their compelling need for egg and sausage sandwiches.

"If it's as late as you say, then it's starting to get early," a gentleman in a sport coat with elbow patches reasoned. "So why can't I get any goddam breakfast?"

Ben's interrogation of the night crew revealed that the problem had started at the drive-thru window.

"Are you sure you should be driving?" Laura had quizzed any customer who slurred his order for "Coffee. Black. Large."

"Can I call someone for you?" Laura had asked. "Why don't you just pull up over there and come in for some coffee? There's a crowd in here tonight and you might run into a friend or two. Wouldn't that be nice?"

Ben wanted to fire her. She was clearly not Burger Meister material. He had started his "it's just not working out" speech, when Laura interrupted, declaring herself solely responsible for the incident and apologizing. Ben looked into her eyes and thought of a great aunt of his who, although in her seventies, was still cleaning other people's houses for the money and not, as his mother often said, because she saw it as her mission to make bathrooms sparkle.

Then Laura politely asked if she still didn't have a couple of weeks of probation left.

"Well, all right," Ben sighed and announced that in roughly five and a half hours, she would begin working the drive-thru window for the early morning shift.

"And remember," he added. "'Efficiency and Courtesy, Fast and Friendly.' Burger Meister customers want their orders filled quickly and they want to see a friendly face—well, don't worry about that part—but you do have to be quick."

By her second day on the morning shift, Laura could tell which customers were in the biggest hurry. Some thrummed their fingers impatiently on their steering wheels; others muttered comments they thought she couldn't hear, or perhaps hoped she could. "Oh Jeez, let's go already," was one of the most frequently heard. *These people in particular need a few words of kindness,* Laura thought. *They are too tense.*

Off on Wednesday, Laura treated herself to a trip to the zoo, a silly indulgence, she thought, but she felt she'd earned it. Once again, she admired the majesty of giraffes in motion. What would it feel like to move like that? So sure-footed and with a slow rhythm that rippled through the anatomy. *Wouldn't we all be happier if we just slowed down a little? "Efficiency and Courtesy, Fast and Friendly." Why aren't courtesy and friendliness enough?*

24

After a sip of coffee, Eleanor watched the tallest giraffe take one slow, delicate step after another across the yard. He had a face as kind as a cat, and just by watching him, she was soothed. Dan was like that, she remembered. They'd both been students at East Liverpool High School, just one year apart, but before he had even noticed her, she had chosen him. It happened during a choir concert. In the audience, Laura had been slouching in her seat when she noticed Dan on stage, the tallest boy in the back row. He was almost a head taller than the boy standing next to him. In the dim light, listening to the choir work their way through a medley from *The Wizard of Oz*, Laura straightened her spine and pulled her shoulders back.

Now she gazed at the tallest giraffe and thought, "Maybe it's not that I'm too slow."

The next morning at the drive-thru was especially hectic. Orders backed up, but instead of asking her customer, a man in a new Prius, to pull up to the parking spot directly in front of him, Laura said, "Now, while we're waiting for your order, why don't you tell me how you like that Toyota you got there."

The man smiled and boasted about his car's amazing mileage, awesome sound system, and extended warranty. "Thanks a lot," he said when at last she handed him his bag of food. "And you have a nice day."

"Don't I remember you from the other day?" she asked the next customer. "Have you switched to decaf since you were here last?"

The pleasant young woman behind the wheel of a Ford Escort confided that she and her husband were hoping to start a family, so she thought she'd make some "healthy lifestyle changes."

"Why, that's wonderful, dear," Laura told her. "Good luck to you and if you need any encouragement about that decaf, you just come back here and see me, okay?"

Further down the drive-thru line, Joe Higgins looked in his rearview mirror and winced. A red-faced man in the SUV behind him yanked his vehicle out of the line and stomped on the gas. The man shook his fist and sounded his horn in one long, angry blast. Tires squealed as he hit the street.

Well, the guy does have a point, Joe thought. *What's taking so long?* He looked at his watch and then glanced at the passenger seat where he'd placed the tools of his trade: a clipboard with several forms, two freshly sharpened number two pencils, and a stopwatch. Joe watched the seconds slip by and sighed.

Moments later, in a parking lot across the street, Joe puzzled over his paperwork. *Employee filled the order quickly.* He was going to have to check the No box on that one, he realized, but that wouldn't tell the whole story. There's not enough space on the form for the whole story. He'd already checked the Yes box in front of *Employee greeted driver,* but she hadn't just greeted him. She'd looked into his eyes, smiled, and asked if he was from out of town. By the time his food arrived he'd told her that he was an efficiency consultant for a large corporation, but that lately the work had been unsatisfying. She had wished him a good day as she handed him his order, the same egg and sausage sandwich, orange juice (large), and coffee (regular) he'd ordered at various Burger Meisters across the Eastern Midwest district hundreds of times before. Then she said she hoped he would find work that was meaningful to him, a job he could look forward to going to everyday. And here was the thing Joe wished he could write on the form: she seemed to mean it when she wished him well. Perhaps if he went through the line again, she'd revert to the cold smile spackled over indifference that typically earned high marks on the employee performance assessment form.

I'll order hash browns and hot chocolate this time, and I bet she won't remember I was just here, he thought, as he turned his car back toward the drive-thru.

"There's this older woman at store 437 who talks to people. I mean she really talks to them, and she makes friends with the customers right there at the drive-thru window," Joe's district manager told his boss over a working lunch the next week. "Can you believe it?"

A few days later, at a meeting of Burger Meister's regional vice presidents, the CEO listened to a report on the impact of his senior hiring plan. "Since employing more seniors, worker high jinks—ice fights, bun battles, and so forth—are at an all-time low," one VP explained, using a laser pointer to indicate a graph on the screen. "However," he paused long enough for everyone at the conference table to look at him, "employee turnover has risen by fourteen point five percent, principally in the teen population. And of those teen workers remaining on the job, forty-three percent report that they are mildly or highly dissatisfied with the recent change. Teen workers just don't want to work alongside their elders, it seems. To quote one sixteen-year-old: 'Just 'cause they're old, they think they can tell us what to do.'"

The CEO ran a hand through his gray hair and looked down at the copy of the report in front of him. For a moment, the room was silent.

At the end of the table, the Regional Vice President for the Eastern Midwest stirred himself to speak.

"Uh, I've gotten reports about a woman at store 437— that's in Ohio—who talks to customers," he says. "You know, one of those new hires. She's quite a hit. People come there just to talk to her. And they buy product too, of course, while they're there."

The CEO looked up. The corners of his mouth rose slightly. "Tell me more," he said.

"I have seen the future," the CEO proclaimed a week later in a special session of the executive board. "And the future of fast food is slowing down. The public is ready for a change, and we at BMC are going to give it to them. Rather than trying to be quicker or trendier than the other guy, we'll be friendlier. We'll give people a fast-food experience that isn't so impersonal, so they'll have a reason to become regulars."

"Gentlemen," and here the CEO paused long enough to beam at each person in the room, "Burger Meister is gone. We are rebranding everything. I present a radical new development in the food service industry: the not-so-fast fast-food restaurant." With a flourish, he whisked a velvet cloth from the easel beside him to reveal a large sign with bold blue lettering–GOOD FOOD, GREAT FOLKS.

It's another Wednesday morning and Laura is at a zoo enjoying the giraffes. *The coffee is better here*, she observes, *but the giraffes are much like the ones back home*. She looks down at the planner in her lap. Next month she'll be vacationing at an animal preserve in Kenya. There is a hotel right on the grounds, and you can enjoy a meal in the second-story dining room while friendly giraffes poke their heads through the open windows. She's seen the pictures on the Internet. Between now and then she'll lead a series of training workshops for the Good Food, Great Folks employees here in Denver, move on to San Diego to visit *that* zoo, and then fly to Las Angeles to tape two new Great Food, Good Folks commercials. She's still startled when she sees herself on television in her hotel suites during these training trips, but she's always pleased to note that the new hairstyle compliments her, the tailored pants suit fit her well, and that she always stands up straight as she invites viewers to "Come on in and make some friends down at our nearest Good Food, Great Folks restaurant."

Laura sips her coffee, and smiles at a trio of giraffes who amble in her direction.

THE REMEDY FOR LOVE

Just because you're old, people think you don't want the candy. So, when they throw it toward the curb, they aim at the children. Or perhaps they don't even see me and Tess sitting there, two women pushing sixty, sitting on the stone steps of an empty house—foreclosed on, judging by the orange sticker on the front door—and one of us worrying our rough seat will cause hemorrhoids. The candy was tossed by the marchers at this year's Pottery Festival—"The Poverty Festival," Tess calls it—looks like a classy selection. Atomic Fireballs, Smarties, even little boxes of Junior Mints. So far, all Tess and I have gotten is what we get every year: flimsy emery boards with some insurance agency's name on them, flyers urging us to vote for this guy for county commissioner and this other one for state representative, and a persistent ringing in our ears. Fire trucks from nearly every town in the tri-state area show up for this parade, sirens all going at once. Dogs howl and the grown-ups plugs their ears and grin. Little kids jump around like they're Frankenstein's monster zapped with a million volts, and between the uproar and all that candy, I'm not sure this is a safe place for children.

"What if," I shout at Tess over the chaos, "what if ten or twenty years from now scientists discover that these are the precise conditions that create serial murderers?"

"Or politicians," Tess adds.

A high school marching band slumps by, struggling through a lethargic rendition of "Hang On, Sloopy," and I realize my head is killing me. Tess seems oblivious to the noise, but she sure loves the political flyers. She delights in tearing them up the second after some grinning fool with a colorful tee shirt admonishing everybody to vote for good ole so-and-so hands her one. I'm grateful the hander-outers are too fast for her. They've already moved on by the time she's shredded the flyer into a dozen pieces, so they miss what's she's done. She sticks the scraps in my purse. And why my purse? Because she hasn't got one. She never carries one and if anyone is so silly as to give her one, she sells it on eBay. Or rather, she *tries* to sell it. Hardly anything Tess puts on eBay sells though. She asks too much, I keep telling her, holds them too dear, as my grandmother used to say. So eventually she gives them away. Not to me, of course, not even if I've admired them. No, they go to the Goodwill. And I go home from the parade with a purse full of trash and zero candy.

Don't think I don't object to Tess using me to haul her garbage every year, because I do.

"I told you, Sarah. I need those scraps for a collage I'm going to make," she says, to keep me from dumping them in the first trash can I see. "I'm going to make a collage full of biting political commentary, and I'm going to enter it in the River Arts Show and show them all what's what."

She says that but she never does it. I don't count it as a mark against her character, because when you know Tess as well as I do, you can tell the difference between the silly ideas she says she's going to put into action and the serious things she pledges to do. The serious things she does.

One of the highlights of this year's parade are the llamas. At least Tess and I, as extra grumpy as she is today, can agree on that. They are splendid. There're eight of them, and each is led by a young man or woman who looks like they'd rather be nowhere else. As for the llamas, they seem surprised to see all of us there on the sidewalk. It's an effect caused by those huge eyes and their magnificent lashes, I suppose. I almost tell Tess how beautiful they look, but I've known her for decades—my god, more than four of them now—and I know she hates beauty. Or at least she hates when people declare that something is beautiful. "How do you know?" She demands. "What is beauty?"

The absolute stars of the parade are two gawky girls on the edge of adolescence walking a Jack Russell terrier who hops on his hind legs. Not such a big trick really, but the fact that the dog is wearing a pink poodle skirt, like something you'd see in the Fifties or on *Happy Days*, makes it funny. Everybody laughs when the dog, still hopping, does a couple of spins on command, and that includes the girls. They giggle, each covering her mouth with a hand, while the crowd guffaws. It's hard to tell at first which is funnier: the girls giggling at their own joke, or the dog, or just the fact that at that one moment, we are all laughing—all the kids, the dads yoked by toddlers on their shoulders, the moms with strollers. Inch by inch, the crowd comes to life as the girls and dog pass by, and laughter sweeps along the street like a pleasant aroma.

"Look at them," Tess says. "Were we ever that unself-conscious? Did we ever let ourselves do something as silly as walk a poodle-skirted dog through a parade? They're beautiful, those two, but I bet they don't know it. I bet they think their feet are too big or maybe they're already afraid their breasts won't be big enough."

Tess has this remarkable way of finding pain in any situation.

After the parade, we drive up St. Clair Avenue for lunch, but then decide we'd rather eat among the smokers across the river. You can still smoke in restaurants in West Virginia. Neither of us smokes, but we like to think of ourselves as daring women, as women who live at least a little dangerously. So, I turn the car around, and this takes us past the Lots & Lots store for the second time which prompts Tess to mention her dream job. For years, she's been saying that the best job in the world would be at PhotoMat.

"It'd be so easy," Tess says now. "Just sit there and wait for someone to pull up and ask for their pictures. Simple really. And pleasant. It'd be like sitting in your own dollhouse, and I could read while I waited, and if it got cold, I'd bring a space heater and maybe have a fridge for my iced tea and...."

There once was a PhotoMat booth in the parking lot of the Lots & Lots, but it's been gone for years. Scraped away. Wouldn't have taken much to plow it down. And Tess has a job. She's the director of an agency that helps needy people—we're an economically depressed Appalachian county here—get to college. She's always frazzled about grants and funding, as well as managing the counseling and tutoring that helps students stay in school.

I'm a librarian.

I can't help but wonder why the lost dream of the PhotoMat has been resurrected today.

"Maybe you could be a greeter at the Lots & Lots," I suggest. "Nothing could be easier than that."

Instantly, Tess has twenty reasons why that job is abysmally inferior to PhotoMat.

"You have to smile at people, you have to stand, you have to shove shopping carts towards people in a nonaggressive manner...." She goes on and on. "Besides, I think I'm still a little too young to take that job."

"Something to look forward to then," I say, and she at least smiles. "Well, okay, how about one of those jobs where you stalk shoppers. You know, where you pretend to be a shopper too, but you're really looking for shoplifters. There's a name for it. Loss something."

"Loss?"

"Loss... loss... Loss Prevention Specialist. That's it." I'm pleased that my memory has coughed up this tidbit on the spot, instead of during some sleepless night three weeks from now.

Tess sits quietly.

"I think I need one of those," she says finally. "I don't want to be one. I don't want to hassle twelve-year-olds stealing blue nail polish—"

"Or old guys sticking steaks down their pants, or—"

"—but I think *I* need a Loss Prevention Specialist. Someone assigned to me full-time who'll follow me around warding off loss."

I know what she means. Tess' first husband died years ago in an accident at the mill. Crushed. God. A couple years after that her only sibling, Susan, died of cancer. And then just a few weeks ago, Susan's husband Frank died up in Cleveland. Another cancer. Pancreatic. Fast.

We decide on Carla's Country Kitchen. We head down the hill and cross the bridge, turn left at the World's Largest Teapot, remnant of an amusement park that closed down about 100 years ago, and there we are. Carla's is in the middle of a block anchored by a Dairy Queen on one end and a boarded-up auto parts store on the other. It has all the mammoth potholes of a really popular truck stop, and the building is large, vast beyond measure. "You could hold a roller derby in the women's room alone," Tess always says. The food is only so-so, but the place is so spacious there are always empty seats, so you can sit forever with a drink and a grilled cheese sandwich, and no one would ever suggest you leave. The waitress would just come by every twenty minutes or so and refill your cup.

We enjoy loitering in Carla's. My favorite booth is the one across from a giant poster of Johnny Cash, leering darkly. There are other posters of country music stars on the walls. At least I think they're music stars. Except for Johnny, they're all young with flowing blonde manes, each of them giving the camera a sidelong smirk. And there's a half dozen TVs on poles throughout the dining room. Today the TVs are all on a game show and blaring a mixture of the emcee's patter and audience applause. I'm a *Judge Judy* person myself, so I don't recognize the game show.

When the waitress brings our drinks, Tess reaches over to get a packet of sugar for her iced tea. She drinks it year round, no matter how cold the weather. If she were on the Titanic, there's no doubt she would wave away a lifejacket, find a waiter, and request just one more glass of iced tea before the ship went down.

"You could bowl in this room," Tess says, gazing around as if this is the first time we've been at Carla's.

"You could hold *league* bowling in here," I add.

33

"*Championship* league bowling," Tess answers. "With rows and rows of bleachers for spectators."

"And still have room left over."

Tess is still shaking the sugar packet when I notice some writing on it.

"Let me see," I say, and she hands it over. I read it and laugh. Someone has written a quote in tidy block lettering: "*Love is the triumph of imagination over intelligence.*"—H.L. Mencken. I read it aloud to Tess and she laughs. Not surprising since after her first husband's death, she's been divorced twice and had a few near misses in between. All of them mistakes to hear her tell it, and she says she is definitely through. No kids though, her choice. "The one thing I did right," Tess always says.

I've got three sons, grown and gone, and Ted, my husband, died five years ago. His first and last heart attack. Boom.

We like to think of ourselves as strong independent women, as survivors.

I pick up another sugar packet and find this: "You can't have everything. Where would you put it?"—Steven Wright.

"Oh, God, yes." Tess laughs out loud at that one. The ways in which we are plagued by our stuff is a common subject for us. Both of us collect things. Depression glass, for example. She's saving a pink pattern called Mayfair, and I'm after a green one called Princess. We also save old postcards, tin toys, McCoy pottery, any number of things. Over the years, we've spent far too much time at garage sales and flea markets, always on the lookout for something else to buy but never ridding ourselves of anything we already have. We both have the basements and attics to prove it.

I reach again for the sugar and find another quote: "There is no remedy for love but to love more."—Henry David Thoreau.

Neither of us laughs at this. I try to connect my image of Thoreau—the straggly beard, the social consciousness, the time at Walden Pond—to the idea of love. Did he ever love anyone? Anyone other than humankind in some capital H kind of way?

Tess looks lost in thought too.

During a break between TV commercials, I can hear Tom Petty lamenting the fact that the waiting is the hardest part. He sounds far off, as if he's in the next county. A radio in the kitchen, I expect. Tess' fingers fuss with a crack in the formica tabletop. The waitress comes by, coffee in one hand and a pitcher of tea in the other, but we decline. It's getting late. We'd talked about stopping at the Rogers Sale, and it seems like a good idea. Ending our day together this early feels wrong.

"I told you about Josh, right?" Tess says, as we head north to the flea market. Josh is her nephew, the only child of her late sister and the recently deceased Frank.

She hadn't.

"He's been living with his best friend's family since Frank died. So, he could finish high school, graduate and everything, and he did all that, but now he's in trouble. He went past his old house last week and saw that the new owners had moved in."

Jeez, I think.

"So he smashed out the windows. One by one, every single window in the house, front, back, and sides. Shattered."

"Jeez," I say. "What happened?"

"Well, the new family came home while he was still at it. Then the cops showed up and arrested him. And Josh tells the cops that they were his rocks so he could do what he wanted with them. Told them he and Frank had collected them during their camping trips, used them to line the front garden."

"So where is he now?"

"On probation and back at his friend's. But the mom called me yesterday and says she wants him gone. He's too angry, she says. Walks around like a fist. I think she's afraid of him after the windows."

I wait. It's the only way with Tess once she starts talking. So, I wait, but for now she seems to be done.

We arrive at the Rogers Sale. A sign at the entrance proclaims it to be Ohio's Largest Flea Market, a credible claim. I navigate around ruts of dried mud in one of the acres of parking lots while mentally vowing not to buy anything. Not to widen, deepen or in any way increase the burden of my possessions. I'm going to play our game instead. Tess invented it. If price were no object, what one thing would you buy? You decide on your one thing and then defend your choice. We do this in art museums too, and we usually find ourselves laughing about our ludicrous plans to buy a Tiffany window or a Monet landscape. Something to class up the bathroom, we joke.

The sale is going strong, busy with browsers who mill around the outdoor tables laden with the usual fare: lidless cookie jars, Scooby Doo glasses, kitchen blenders that look like their pureeing days are done. To cover more ground, Tess and I go our separate ways, looking over different tables while the dealers slouch in chairs and sip drinks. The day has warmed up considerably since the parade, and sunshine gleams on the curve of a ceramic pitcher, sparkles on a punchbowl full of Christmas ornaments. From here I can smell the hot oil from a nearby french fry wagon. *You just ate*, I remind myself, as I start scanning a new table and see a *Dukes of Hazard* lunchbox beside a stack of *Mad* magazines. *For heaven's sake. How much will they want for this? It's rusty!* Prepared to be appalled, I reach for the lunchbox to check the price when I notice a cardboard box next to it. I stand on my toes to peer down into what looks like a pile of photos.

There's an unframed sepia-toned photograph on top, a formal studio portrait. A young man in World War II army uniform, blonde and handsome, leaning slightly forward. He looks intent, eager, an American youth ready to do what's needed. I turn it over but there's no inscription.

Below it is a black and white snapshot of a younger man in a wide-lapel suit and snappy fedora. He stands with one foot on the running board of an enormous sedan. I hold the photos side by side and yes, it's the same fellow. Pure boyish joy in the car photo; in the other he's been made serious by—what? The passing of a few years? The war? The photographer's instructions?

I look up and spot Tess a few feet away. She's scrounging through a box on the ground. "Never forget to look on the ground" is her motto. She can tell you tales about fine stuff she's found in boxes half-shoved under tables. I call her over and, like a pair of archeologists, we start sifting through the layers. Tess finds a greeting card. "Phillip" someone has written above the printed message. "Happy Birthday, Sweetheart." No signature.

So, this is Phillip.

"Yeah, isn't that something?" The dealer, a heavy-set young man with a ponytail heaves himself out of a chair and meanders over. "It was in a load of stuff I got from another guy. I wanted ten, but I'll take eight for it. The whole thing."

I pull out more photos. In one, two little girls with crooked bangs perch on merry-go-round horses. They're grinning at the photographer, an expression that reveals that both are missing a front tooth. Phillip's daughters? Again, there's no inscription, no hint of the date or identities.

The dealer moves on down to another table where a man is holding a *Life* magazine aloft and seems to have a question.

A nightclub photo is next. Phillip is in uniform again, but this time he's smiling broadly, one arm around a woman with Veronica Lake hair, a curtain of curl covering one eye. Cocktail glasses sit on the table in front of them. Maybe this is Phillip's wife, the mother of the two girls. Or a wartime sweetheart.

"Eight bucks, Sarah," Tess says. We exchange a look. I can picture the two of us spreading out the fragments of Phillip's life on Tess' living room floor, war years on one side, family snapshots on another, piecing together a past, assembling a life. I'm trying to think of something to say, when the dealer returns and stands in front of us. He puts his hands on his hips.

"It's a load of stuff alright. There's even some guy's high school diploma in there. Couple of quality picture frames too."

It's a pig in a poke, my grandmother would say. A thing you should never buy.

"How about it, ladies? How about seven dollars, so I don't have to haul this thing home?"

The comment floats in the air between us. We like to think of ourselves as smart, mouthy women, so I want to say "Mister, we ain't no ladies," but I don't.

The man gives his ponytail a tug and looks vaguely toward the french fry wagon before turning back to us. "Six is as low as I can go," he says. "How about it?"

Tess always says silence is her best negotiating strategy. Silence and a little time. We look at each other again. I don't need any frames. Got a crate full of perfectly usable ones in the garage. And as for photos, aside from the two on my desk and the few that made it into albums when the boys were young, I've got hundreds residing in a plastic tub in the spare room. The irony of this pull to adopt Phillip's disjointed life while my own family memorabilia is neglected does not escape me.

"Let's get out of here before we buy this box and become amateur curators," I say.

Tess tells the man "No thanks," and we head for the parking lot.

"What have you got on for tomorrow?" I ask Tess on the drive to her house. Tomorrow is Sunday, another day off work. I have lots to do around the house, laundry included, but I don't want to do any of it. Another day before Monday, and then another week of story hours, of helping patrons find the one mystery in our little library that they haven't already read, of hearing again that it's a crying shame the library ever got rid of the card catalog. The most creative task I have coming up this week is dismantling the pottery exhibit in the big display case and replacing it with Mrs. Neville's—one of our favorite patrons—collection of Amish dolls. Although I can empathize with a fellow collector, I can't help but wonder why anyone would want more than one faceless doll in a black dress. Still, I'll happily arrange the dolls as artfully as possible because I've long ago run out of ideas for the display case.

"I might be driving to Cleveland," Tess says as she gets out of the car.

As she walks to her door, I catch myself thinking that if it's Phillip's high school diploma in that box, it would have his full name on it. I could google him. And if he's dead—and most likely he is dead—there'd be an obit. Perhaps there are survivors. The

38

girls on the merry-go-round, or the Veronica Lake lady, or grand-children. Someone may want that box.

I imagine myself phoning someone who remembers Phillip fondly, who tears up when I arrive at some restaurant lugging the box to place in their eager hands. But if there's no one, or if the only people left are estranged from Phillip and only want to tell me what a monster he was before they hang up on me, then what?

I imagine myself arranging Phillip's photos and cards and diplomas in the library display case. I could make a sign: Don't Let This Happen to You.

I imagine myself slowly unpacking the box's contents, methodically laying each item down, like tarot cards that could reveal a story, a message.

And then I remember a visit I once made to the Johnstown Flood Museum and a ceiling-high display made up of items scattered by the flood, items picked up after the waters receded. It was one thing to see before and after photos of the flood's destruction, to read the telegraph message sent to Pittsburgh—"Send coffins. All sizes."—but the hair combs and bottles, the toy top, the ring, the doll's head, the commonplace leftovers of ordinary lives testified to the devastation in an entirely different way. I saw a news story years ago after a tornado. I can't remember which one. A group of people collected family photos that had been picked up by the winds and strewn across miles of countryside. Those people laid the photos out on long, long tables in a school gymnasium and invited the public to walk up and down the aisles, studying the photos so they could claim what was theirs, what they surely thought had been forever lost.

As if by itself, the car pulls into a driveway.

Why shouldn't I devote the library display case to Phillip?

I back into the street, turning around.

In fact, why not a museum?

I head for the stop sign, but somehow drive right through.

Why shouldn't there be an entire museum that features Phillip at first, but then exhibits artifacts from some other lost soul the next month, and another the following month, and so on? There might be no end to it.

I ignore the blaring horn and screeching brakes as a car avoids hitting me. My foot presses the gas pedal. I head back to Rogers.

I hope I'm in time.

THE SECRET OF FLOATING

"There's a dead guy in that pot."

Bevie and Tommy are riding their bikes through the cemetery when Bevie remembers a book she saw in the library a few days ago. One picture in particular struck her, a photograph of a pot found in a cave, and in it, a dead man curled up like a dried earthworm.

"There's a man in there," Bevie says again, stopping her bike. "Well, a body." She points to a tall stone urn that sits atop a family plot marked "Vollnagle." Tommy stops too.

"In there?" he frowns. "Naw, they put dead people in the ground."

"This is different," Bevie says and tells him about the book. She's been spending a lot of time with books this summer, skimming through them in the cool basement room that is the children's department of the library. She is there so often, in fact, that the librarian has taken notice. Lately, she has pursued Bevie with one relentless theme: there are certain books girls Bevie's age really should read. A few days earlier Bevie was scanning the shelves for books about dinosaurs as the librarian campaigned on behalf of Louisa May Alcott. As she followed Bevie with a copy of *Little Women* in hand, Bevie pulled her hand across sweaty bangs and drew from the shelf a thin book called *The Story of Early Man*. No dinosaurs there. In spite of what Bevie had seen in cartoons, she knew that Early Man hadn't been around to thrust spears into tyrannosauruses. But there were illustrations that caught her interest, including a series of drawings of Early Man spread across

41

two pages. In it, Early Man seemed to walk from the left side of the book to the right with his brow becoming less prominent, his spine a bit straighter as he went. Towards the end of the book there was a photograph: "Early Man discovered in his grave." A man in a pot.

"Naw, they put bodies in the ground," Tommy insists. "I went to my grandmother's funeral and watched them. Her body was in a coffin, and then they closed the coffin and drove it to the cemetery, and then they put the coffin in the ground—with her in it. I was right there. I saw it."

"Well, why is this pot here then?" Bevie has never seen a dead body or been to a funeral, but she has seen that book. This pot is shaped just like the one in the picture, wide for most of its height and narrow at the top. "Look, I'll show you."

They can reach the top of the pot if they stand on their toes, but to investigate thoroughly, to peer inside, requires a greater height, so Tommy hoists her up. Like Bevie, Tommy is 9, but he is the smallest boy in his fourth-grade class and only a fraction of an inch taller than Bevie. He is a frail looking child that most of the other kids don't like. They make fun of his flannel shirts with pictures of cowboys, Indians, and blazing six guns on them. But Bevie does not hold that against him. Her mother never buys her the clothes she wants either. For instance, the swimsuit her mother selected for her this summer has a leopard print. "I thought you liked animals," her mother said when Bevie frowned.

Tommy holds Bevie's waist and lifts her as she grasps the pot near its top. As her hands glide up its sun-warmed sides, she feels uneasy. The pot in the book looked rough and scratchy, and this one is slippery smooth.

"Well?" Still holding her, Tommy leans against the pot for support. Bevie takes her look inside just as a knot of doubt grips her chest. A layer of cement covers the opening, and she reaches in to touch it.

"Let me down," she says, and when he does, she tries to lift him. Mostly he pulls himself up to the urn's edge. *The color is wrong,*

Bevie thinks. This pot is pink, not a baby girl pink but a dusty pink, with black streaks and sprinklings of a sparkly silver. In the photograph, Early Man's pot had looked as brown as the dirt of his cave, as mud colored as his leathery skin.

"See, I told you," Tommy says, now back on his feet and grinning at her. "He's in the ground just like the rest of them. I don't care what the book says."

Bevie, who cares a great deal what books say, gets back on her bike and together they pedal to the swimming pool.

Bevie didn't have to do anything to become Tommy's friend. When she moved to Madison Hill Road with her parents at the start of school last year, she made, at her mother's urging, an attempt at a friendship with the twin girls who lived in the house next door. But all they wanted to do was sew clothes for their Barbies. It wasn't long before Bevie drifted to the other end of the dead-end street and the Capaldis, a family with five boys. Tommy seemed eager to play with anyone who wasn't one of his brothers. The eldest was Patrick, a high school student who seldom smiled and rarely spoke; Galen was 11 and twice Bevie's size; four-year-old Nicky spent a lot of time pretending to be a dog; and Gabriel was the baby that Bevie had never seen outside of the house. She immediately took to Tommy, who was only a couple of months younger than her. He always looked as if his clothes hadn't made a trip to the laundry room before being handed down to him. And he was the friendliest of the Capaldi bunch, except for Nicky who grinned every time one of his bothers shouted, "Good dog!" He took this as his signal to drop to all fours, paw at the ground, and bark joyfully.

Bevie and Tommy's friendship had been sealed that Spring with their discovery of a fossil. Bevie had been reading about dinosaurs and decided that the field that ran in a wide strip behind both of their houses was, without doubt, a dinosaur graveyard. They poked around with their fathers' shovels for a couple of afternoons and discovered what might have been the fossil of a fern frond. The fossil was at the edge of one corner of a large rock more than twice the size of her mother's briefcase. It was a bit like the Shroud of Turin, obvious only to anyone who came prepared to see it. Galen spotted it right away but was not impressed. "Of course, it's a fossil. So what?" Patrick snorted and walked away, but that was his reaction to everything. Once it was placed on the ground in front of Nicky, he sniffed at it and barked. Bevie's mother, on the other hand, studied the rock from various angles and looked puzzled. There might be a fossil there, she allowed, but she couldn't see it. As Bevie told her father about the fossil when he called her that Thursday night, he chuckled and suggested they keep digging. Tommy's father was rarely home and missed the opportunity to weigh in with an opinion. Only Mrs. Capaldi was effusive. It was a fine fossil, she exclaimed, and she was proud of both of them for being clever enough to find it.

Bevie and Tommy quickly decided that the fossil would have to be taken to school. In fact, Bevie had already talked up the ongoing project of unearthing a dinosaur that was surely in the field waiting for them, so here would be solid evidence that they were nearing their goal. The only problem was that the fossil was part of such a large and hefty rock. As obstinate as stone herself, Bevie vetoed any thought of breaking the rock into a more manageable size.

"That's too risky," she declared. "What if we damage it?" Instead, she insisted they place their treasure in a shallow cardboard box and, with one of them on each side, carry it down Madison Hill to the bus stop. Together they hoisted it aboard the bus where Mr. Jenkins, the driver, who had seen far more interesting specimens than this lugged to school over the years, refused to admire it. Patrick pretended not to know them, while some of the other riders craned to see it but quickly lost interest. Once at school, they struggled it off the bus, into the building, and down to Bevie's classroom before the first bell. When they pushed and shoved the box down to Tommy's classroom immediately after school, his teacher was even more skeptical than Bevie's had been.

44

The fossil hadn't exactly met with acclaim from Bevie's classmates either. In fact, no one's enthusiasm for the fossil came anywhere near Tommy and Bevie's.

Weary of skeptics, the two friends wrangled their mutual burden out to the front of the school where they discovered they had just missed the bus home. Mrs. Capaldi didn't drive, and the other parents were at work, so walking was their only option.

They carried the stone out the school drive and then up Park Avenue, stopping frequently to stand up straight, stretch their backs, and catch their breath, swapping sides before heading down Elm Street. Next came the encouraging downhill slope of Pittsburgh Street, but that left them at the bottom of Madison, facing the hill. Bevie cajoled, badgered, and nagged Tommy and the stone up their street and onto a place of pride on a shelf in her parent's garage.

Their long-term plan, they had decided on the long trek home, was to convert the garage into a museum for all their future finds. But after several afternoons of digging that yielded nothing—and one unpleasant experience with a snapping turtle they tried to catch in the tiny pond in their dinosaur field—they lost interest in fossils and dinosaurs. By then summer had arrived and with it the reopening of the park swimming pool.

The best way to get to the pool from Bevie's house was to ride the narrow path through the field, past the snapping turtle pond, and then through the cemetery to Park Avenue. Once at Park, Bevie glanced quickly up and down the street, dashed across, and shoved her bike across the grass. Grasshoppers leapt wildly in front of her. After thrusting the bike into the rack outside the pool and flashing her season pass at the high school girl who sat reading a Stephen King paperback at the cashier's booth, Bevie walked into the women's dressing room. Already she could smell the eye-burning scent of bleach.

Once inside the pool area, Bevie walked past Tommy who was standing at the baby end, strode confidently to the six-foot marker, and without hesitation, jumped in, hugging her knees to maximize the impact. She swam around the deep end for awhile. She could see Tommy frowning as he crept cautiously into the pool at the baby end, stopping when the water reached his chest.

Why did he come along? It was clear to see that he didn't really like to swim. He'd been riding his bike to her house every day recently, just hanging around.

"Do you want to ride over to Sinclair's Dairy and get a root beer popsicle?"

"No, thank you," she said.

"To Ryan News for a Superman comic?"

"No, I would not." She'd rather stay inside and read, but she didn't say so. Company wasn't allowed inside unless her mother was home, so she was stuck outside with Tommy.

Yesterday they had been sitting on Bevie's front lawn while Tommy told her about the Dracula movie he'd seen. He was describing the end, about how the good guys found Dracula in his coffin and what they had to do to make him really dead, when Bevie's mother came home from work.

"Summer will be over before you know it," her mother said as she swung her legs out of the car. "You shouldn't be spending your summer vacation moping around the house. One of these fine days you'll be sitting in school wishing you'd done something with this time while you had it." She reached into the back seat for her briefcase, straightened up, and faced Bevie. "Why aren't you going to the pool? Your father bought you that season pass on the condition that you would use it, remember?"

Somehow, in the few steps from the driveway to the back door, plans were made. The very next day, Tommy would come over after lunch and together he and Bevie would ride their bikes to the pool.

Bevie swam toward Tommy and splashed him, commencing a splash battle, with each of them creating tidal waves by moving their arms as fast and hard as they could across the top of the water. After the war Bevie suggested penny diving. For a nonswimmer, Tommy was surprisingly good at this. They took turns tossing the penny a couple of feet in front of them, then surface dived and reached through the swirling sediment, the grit washed off the sweaty bodies of a hundred children. Each grasped the coin and resurfaced, holding it high like deep sea adventurers retrieving doubloons.

Confident that she had the advantage, Bevie challenged Tommy to a floating contest. She knows the secret of floating—her father had taught it to her last summer—and the secret is this: surrender.

"People think the secret is to relax," Bevie explained to Tommy. "But if someone tells you to relax, you usually do the opposite, you tense up." Bevie could even see her advantage over Tommy. Each time he tried to stretch out onto the water, he tightened his jaw and wrinkled his brow, and each effort ended in wild thrashing. Tommy soon gave up and stood by Bevie, giving her an embarrassed smile as he coughed and wiped water from his eyes.

Then it was Bevie's turn. As if the water would solidify beneath her, she lay back, and then she was on, in, and of the water all at once. This was her favorite part: the first seconds of floating, the first tickle of water in her ears, the shudder that passes through her body, the feeling of calm that seemed to warm her. Then came the deafening of sound, of all the kids yelling to each other and the crackle of the radio station over the loudspeaker. And finally, an awareness of new sounds: her own slow breathing—surprisingly steady and strong—and liquid, gurgling noises from below. She opened her eyes and saw, above her, above all of them, all the kids and all their noisome fun, a cloudless blue sky and, peripherally, a dark fringe of pines, like sentries standing watch just outside the pool's fence.

Miss Beverly Everly, Bevie sang to herself as she floated. *Who does everything so cleverly. Will I ever stop loving you? Neverly.* Her father had made that up and sung it to her at bedtime for as long as she could remember. And last summer he had stopped at the pool every afternoon on his way home from work to pick her up. He'd stand on the outdoor deck and watch while she'd demonstrate some new trick she'd learned, like turning a somersault under water. But after Christmas he had moved out of their house and into an apartment two states away. Now she had to wait until Thursday nights to talk to him on the phone. "Miss Beverly Everly," he'd sing to her from miles and miles away. "Will I ever stop loving you?"

Bevie sang her father's song over and over until a whistle shrieked and the lifeguard yelled, "Clear the pool! Everybody out!" At the pool's edge she found Tommy.

"Hey, I brought money," he said. "Let's get something."

High school girls were selling pretzel rods, tiny bags of potato chips, and frozen Snicker bars from a pair of windows at the far side of the pool house. Tommy and Bevie joined the long line of wet children who are wrapped in towels and clutching coins. Some shivered. In front of them, a small boy with dark curls shook his head like a dog emerging from a lake, and two blonde girls with matching polka dot swimsuits shrieked with delight.

"Hey, Jane," a voice from behind them called. Bevie looked up to watch the lifeguard who slowly removed her sunglasses and whistle and set them on her tall, tall chair. Somewhere behind Bevie a girl giggled.

"Hey, Ja-a-ane!" Louder now. Bevie wondered, *Is he talking to me?* She turned to look behind her and saw Ricky, a sixth grader, looking right at her, a malicious grin broadening his face. Giggling and leaning on his arm was Vicki Anderson who seemed much older than Bevie in a two-piece swimsuit the color of the sky, her brown hair held back with a matching scarf.

Turning away from Vicki, Bevie watched as the lifeguard stood at the deep end of the pool. The guard tilted her head from one side to another as she tucked her hair into a swim cap. Then she paused, poised at the edge of the pool, and dove effortlessly, her white swimsuit reflecting the sun and the almost blinding sparkle of the water.

"Jane! Yeah, you—Queen of the Jungle."

Shut up, Bevie thought. She wanted to glare at Ricky, but she could feel her face reddening and decided to ignore him.

"Hey, Jane, is that Tarzan there with you?"

It's the swimsuit, and these dumb leopard spots. Angry now, she turned to stare at Ricky who leered at her. He made a face at Vicki who giggled even more. Behind Vicki, Bevie saw the laughing face of Gary, Ricky's friend.

"Naw, that's Cheetah," said Gary. Gary and Ricky made monkey sounds and scratched their armpits. Vicki laughed.

Shut up, Bevie wanted to say. *Shut your ugly mouths.* Behind her she heard Tommy breathing, but she couldn't make herself look at him. Instead, she willed herself to watch the lifeguard. The guard swam almost the entire length of the empty pool in one smooth seamless underwater effort, her arms pulling her through, her body straight and purposeful. Slowly she emerged at the shallow end, where she stood for a moment, peeling back the swim cap.

As if she didn't just do something wonderful, Bevie thought.

Later, Tommy and Bevie got Dilly Bars and sat on the grass in front of the Dairy Queen trying to finish them before they slipped off the sticks. The afternoon sun cast shadows behind them.

"That guy is under the cement, you know," Tommy said. "They couldn't let him sit in there without some kind of lid on the pot. Maybe he felt funny being buried in the ground. So they put him in the pot and then poured cement on the top so nobody could steal him." Tommy looked thoughtfully at his empty Dilly Bar stick. "Yeah, he's all sealed up, but he's in there all right."

Bevie pulled up her knees and hugged her thin legs. She could still smell the swimming pool on her arms, and she thought about how different this summer was from last summer. *Everything changes. Next summer will be different too.* She inspected her fingertips, still wrinkled from an afternoon in the water.

Tommy didn't come to Bevie's house the next day. He wasn't there the day after that either, so after lunch, Bevie rode up

49

the street. No bikes were strewn across the Capaldi's front lawn, and the garage door was up, revealing an emptiness that startled her. After she looked through the living room window and saw that the furniture too was gone, Bevie rode her bike to the park alone.

What happened? Where have they gone? How could Tommy just disappear like that?

In the pool, she floated. *Is this what it's like to die? To lie back while your life fades away? And to finally stop breathing and sink?*

Bevie tried to tune in to the gurgling sounds that rose up from the bottom of the pool. They almost sounded like words, as if people were talking in the next room behind a closed door, adults maybe, parents making plans all their own. Maybe, maybe, if she listened harder she could make sense of them.

And Your Name Is?

Thank you, but no, I never eat potato chips in public. Not since the third grade when the other kids made fun of me. My mother always packed my lunch, see, and sometimes she'd put in a little bag of potato chips for a special treat—DanDee brand potato chips. And since my name was DeeDee, the other kids started calling me DanDee and I hated it. I wanted to change my name, but I couldn't. I was just a kid. So, I told my mother that the potato chips made me sick, hoping she'd stop buying them. Eventually the kids stopped teasing me, but even so, I could never eat potato chips again. At least not in public. But thanks anyway.

See, the problem with DeeDee is that it sounds like a nickname for something longer—Dorothy, maybe, or Diana—but it was my real name. It's not an awful name. I don't fault my parents any. It's just that it's such a young name. DeeDee sounds like the girl who sits next to you in biology that you invite to your sleepover. Or the babysitter you hire to stay with the kids while you go out to a movie. Not a terrible name, it's just that I got older than it.

The year I turned fifty I thought about what present I might give myself and it occurred to me that I could change my name. I got to thinking about this when I was talking to a friend of mine, Lorraine Wilkins. She goes to our church and on the weekends she waitresses at Carla's Country Kitchen, right across the river. Dick and I love to go there and sit at one of her tables because we don't even have to ask, she will just automatically bring us more of those buttermilk biscuits, and if we don't finish them, she would always say, "Go ahead and take them home. We're just gonna throw them out anyway."

Well, Lorraine has a daughter named Mary Beth. A couple of years ago Mary Beth, who must be about forty now, saw an ad in a magazine that said if you send this man in Arizona $125, he will reveal your true name to you. Now, according to him, your true name is not the one your parents gave you. It's what your name should have been. He claims that just discovering your true name unleashes your personal power and enhances your creativity. So, for a fee he somehow divines what your parents would have named you if they had his sensitivity to names, and then he writes it down and sends it to you. Mary Beth must have shipped off the $125 because shortly after she mentioned this ad to her mother, she started telling everyone that her real name was Bellphoebe Coyote Spencer and not Mary Beth Wilkins.

Anyway, Lorraine complained about this a lot, about how could any child of hers be so foolish as to send $125 to a stranger just to be told something so silly, something he was just making up and all it cost him was the price of a stamp. But while she was complaining, I was wondering, what if this is true? What if we are all supposed to have a certain name, but our parents got it wrong and named us after Uncle Al or Cousin Margaret? Is something in us squashed down, you know, stifled, if we go through life with the wrong name? I was just about to ask Lorraine which magazine Mary Beth found this ad in, when she started complaining about Mary Beth spending hundreds, maybe a thousand dollars, to get all the fillings in her teeth removed because she'd heard somewhere that the metal fillings sap your creative powers, just drained them right out of you. Lorraine said that Mary Beth blamed her because Lorraine had raised her in a backward town that didn't want to add fluoride to the water because two of the councilmen said it was a Communist plot and an especially evil way to undermine Americans. But that was years ago. We've had fluoride for oh, a long time now and I don't see any Communists around, do you?

So, I decided not to ask Lorraine about the ad. Instead, I got a book of baby names from the Friends of the Library's used book sale and flipped through it but didn't like any of the names.

I skimmed through all the female names backwards and forwards and nothing clicked.

Then I tried what my Meemaw used to do with the family Bible. I always wondered about that Bible. You know how the front of a Bible has these pages where you write down important family matters, like births and deaths? Well, when we'd ask Meemaw about who were those people named in our family Bible, she'd say, "Never mind" and change the subject. The names weren't any names we knew, they weren't anybody that Meemaw ever mentioned when she told us family stories. That seemed strange. I talked this over with my older sister Amelia once, years later, and she said that our people probably stole that Bible from somebody else's people on the boat coming over. I'd like to think that it's not true, but....

Where was I? Oh, yes. When Meemaw had a question, like what to do about Grandpa Fred who was such a drinker and always causing trouble, she'd get out the family Bible. She would sit in her chair with the closed Bible on her legs and pray out loud, asking the Lord to show her what she should do. Then she'd close her eyes, open the Bible and point to a verse, open her eyes, and read that verse out loud. She was living with us by then, always cooking cabbage and staring at our friends. Most of the time what she'd read didn't make any sense to us. It didn't seem to have anything to do with Grandpa, but she'd think about if for a couple of days and then, at dinner one night, she'd tell us what she decided it meant. Once I remember her finger landed on one of those long "begetting" parts of the Old Testament, and when we were all at the dinner table next evening, except for my brother Daniel who was in the Army by then, Meemaw said, "The Lord wants me to accept Fred's other children as if they were my own." Well. We all sat there quiet for a long time and then my sister Eileen and I, who were hearing about Grandpa's other family for the very first time, started asking questions. I think we wondered if there were other grandchildren we could play with. We were about 11 and 10, I think, and pretty sick of each other's company.

Eileen and I adored Grandpa because back when we were wee little he used to call us "the twins" and we loved that, but

Amelia, our oldest sister, got angry about Grandpa having another whole family. But what was the point of getting angry about it? He'd already been dead a year. Amelia went on and on, said she'd always suspected he was capable of such a thing. Mother, meanwhile, just stayed quiet. She stared down at the food on her plate, but I could see the sadness in her eyes. She never would talk about it though. Not even after Meemaw died too or even toward the end of her own life.

Now as far as I know, Meemaw never did a thing about that other family, whoever they were. For years though, whenever Eileen and I saw kids about our age we'd say, "Could those be Grandpa's other grandchildren?" We used to make up stories about them and give them crazy, exotic names like Orina or Ariadne. The other grandchildren were always wild, as wild as we would have liked to have been if we had dared, shoplifting toys and candy, and skipping school, and in our stories, they always got away with it. I think we made ourselves jealous of those other grandchildren, which seems odd since they might not have even existed.

So I tried Meemaw's method with *What Shall We Name the Baby?* book, but gave up because it kept opening to the boy baby section and my finger would land on names like Greyson or Bartholomew. After the third try, I forced it to the girls' names and found my finger on Harleen. I took that as a sign that this was not going to work, and I quit. I even donated the book back to the Friends for their next sale.

Well, then I got to thinking why not just drop one of the Dees, so I would be Dee. You know, like Cher is just Cher and Beyonce is Beyonce. I went back to the library and did some research on what you have to do to legally change your name. You have to petition a judge and pay some money. It always comes down to money, doesn't it? But Dick, my husband—Yes! We were Dick and DeeDee, can you believe it? Ever since the 11th grade—he said, "Honey, I could buy you a case of White Out for a lot less money and you could change your name yourself." So, I dropped it, the idea of officially dropping a Dee, that is. And then on my fiftieth birthday, which was a Tuesday, Dick gives me this box wrapped in beautiful paper with the most beautiful pink roses on it and tied with a big pink bow and inside there were twelve bottles of White Out and a note that said, "Let's use the money we saved on your name change to celebrate your birthday in style."

And that's what we did. We took a three-day cruise to the Bahamas and had a terrific time. Between the shows and the island tours, it was great. The trip of a lifetime. One afternoon we were on board and while Dick was taking his nap, I sat at the little desk in our cabin and wrote out postcards to our friends back home and signed them, "Dee." Just Dee. No, I didn't write "just Dee" but you know what I mean.

So, I've been just Dee for five years now. Dick still likes to tease me. "Which Dee did you drop, honey? The first one or the last one?" And Petey, our youngest who was about seventeen at the time, gave me a card that said, "Happy Birthday to The Big D." He said it was very cool to have a letter for a first name just then. I didn't want to tell him that my name is D-E-E and not just the letter D. It's been a very long time since Petey thought that anything I've done was acceptable, let alone cool. Let alone very cool.

Now what was that you were telling me about these potato chips?

Oh, they're on sale? I love a good sale.

CHANCE ENCOUNTER

"Look around," his aunt had said. "Explore the place." Josh must have looked baffled by his Aunt Tess' long recital of the street names and traffic signals he'd come across. Finally, she said, "Just keep going down the hill and stop when you come to the river. The river is a good starting point." So, Josh carefully threaded his way through curving streets narrowed by cars parked along the curb on both sides. And she was right: it *was* all downhill.

After several blocks, it was there before him, what this downward slope had been leading him to—the Ohio River. Josh stopped in front of a boat launch and considered the grey-brown water before him. Except for a few ducks that bobbed at the river's edge—muttering as they jostled each other—and the coal barge that was just passing out of sight, the riverfront was quiet, uninhabited. Josh knew that he'd been here before back when was a little kid, but he couldn't remember any details. And now, because he was more accustomed to the wide expanse of Lake Erie, the river seemed small, and the houses on the West Virginia shore as well as the green hills that rose beyond them seemed remarkably close.

Josh tried to pin down his memory of this river. He seemed to recall a time he was on a boat here. Whose boat would it have been? His aunt hadn't owned a boat, and she was the only person he knew here. But there was something else he remembered, something about being on the river and looking at the unfolding panorama of towns as the boat moved past them. What you saw from the boat, he remembered, was not the public side of a town's buildings, the side you would see as you drove down the town's streets. No, you saw the backs of things, the secret side of the town's houses and stores, its gas stations and schools, a perspective usually available only to the non-stranger. He seemed to remember that during that trip down the river he had invented tiny dramas to go along with the details he had observed—a woman hanging clothes on the line, a dog chained to a doghouse that barked and barked, a little girl swinging on a swing set. Yes, he did have memories of this river.

Once, when Josh was very young, he'd had a fever for a few days. He and his parents had just moved into a new house in a neighborhood that he didn't know. He had gotten ill before he'd had time to explore on his bike. He sat by his bedroom window one day, still weak, and looked across the back yard, past the maple tree and the garden shed, and into the back neighbor's yard. From where he sat, he could see a woman in what must be her kitchen. She seemed to be standing at her sink. In his fever, he began to imagine stories about this unknown woman: she was kind, a fairy tale grandmother who baked cookies and distributed them to all the neighborhood kids, and she loved to plant marigolds along the walk in front of her house. Later, when he was well enough to explore, he'd been disappointed by the front of the neighbor's house. There were weeds where he'd imagined flowers, an unkempt lawn, and a mean looking dog, chained to a stake, who had lunged at him when he walked by. He had gotten it all wrong.

On this day though, his first in this place that was his new home, Josh turned the car around in the boat launch parking lot and headed north a couple of blocks until he saw a small business district. Between The Wandering Sock Laundromat (boarded and closed) and a barber shop with the name too faded to read (also boarded and closed) was the K & L Donut Shop, a parking space in front of it, and inside, open seats at the counter. Once he was inside, a waitress, a petite girl about sixteen, brought him a mug of coffee. Josh unfolded an abandoned newspaper on the counter in front of him and began to read.

"Did you see that one?"

Josh had been reading a letter to the editor where some-one was giving the school board hell for something when a finger jabbed at the newspaper. Josh turned on his stool. A guy about his age, eighteen or so, grinned down. The kid poked again at the right-hand side of the page.

"Did you read it? Pretty funny, huh?"

The kid had dark curly hair and huge teeth. He was tall, at least six foot two, wide shouldered, and still grinning.

"See what?"

"That one there." The kid gestured at the paper again, and Josh read an entry in the Police Blotter:

9:05 p.m. Tuesday: Owner of a Sixth St. residence reports finding 37 grilled cheese sandwiches on her front porch.

"Pretty funny, huh?" The kid chuckled. He looked a little like one of the brothers in the black and white movies Josh used to watch on TV with his dad. He couldn't remember their names. Seating him-self on the stool next to Josh, the curly haired kid grabbed the paper out of his hands, and read the item aloud, slowly, appreciatively.

"Nine oh five p.m...."

Josh remembered that the curly haired man in his dad's favorite movies never talked. The man's curls were lighter than this guy's. Blond maybe. Or red. Who could tell in a movie without color? That was the problem. You could never tell how anything was really supposed to be.

The kid leaned toward Josh and hunched down to say in a husky stage whisper, "Bet the cops are still trying to figure that one out." He handed the paper back to Josh. "So, what d'ya think?"

"It's pretty weird. Why would anyone throw thirty-seven grilled—"

"Exactly!" The kid smacked the palm of his hand on the counter and the waitress, lingering by the donut display case, gig-gled and tucked a lock of hair behind her ear.

58

The brothers in the movies all had names that ended in O, Josh remembered. *Gummo? Bammo? No.*

"Well, what do you think? Why do you think somebody would put a bunch of sandwiches on an old lady's porch?"

"Some kind of prank, I guess." Josh gave it some more thought. *There had to be a reason. There's a reason for everything, or there certainly ought to be.* "Okay, well, maybe the old lady goes to the same restaurant every day for lunch and always gets a grilled cheese sandwich, but she never leaves a tip and the waitress finally gets fed up and drives by the old lady's house and—"

"Hey, that's good." The kid stared at him. "That's pretty good thinking. Okay, but what if that wasn't it though? What if there was some other reason?"

Josh thought some more. It was an interesting puzzle.

"Okay, well, maybe there's these two guys, and they like to prank each other. And one of the guys has all these sandwiches, but he forgets his friend's address and he goes to the wrong house by mistake. If he left the sandwiches on the porch of the right house, well, those people would know it was a joke and might have thought, 'Oh man, Joe got us good this time. We'll have to think of something pretty good to top this.' But they wouldn't call the cops because there wouldn't have been any mystery about it, at least not to them."

The kid leaned away from Josh and raised his eyebrows.

"Hey," he said, stretching the word like it was made of elastic and he wasn't afraid of snapping it. "I like the way you think. But no, that's not it. Nice try though. You really got into the spirit of the thing, and I like that." The kid swiveled on his stool. "Hey, Shannon, what you been up to these days?"

Although she had seemed bored when she brought Josh his coffee, the waitress had been listening from her position by the donut case. Now she glanced at the kid, smiled, and quickly dropped her eyes.

"I was wondering when you were going to speak to me, Chance."

59

"Yeah, well, I've been busy brainstorming with the new guy here."

He asked her something else, but Josh tuned out their conversation. He thought about those old movies, about how his dad would roll his head back and howl at something the brothers did. *In one of the movies, they were trying to move a piano up an impossibly long flight of stairs. No, wait. That wasn't the brothers. That was two other guys in some other movie. The brothers though, the one with the curly hair had a bicycle horn he'd honk whenever a pretty girl walked by. And sometimes he played something, some kind of instrument. A piano maybe? The movie always got a little serious then, like his music was too pretty to laugh about. A few moments of grace in between the mayhem.*

"Hey, you want to know what really happened?" The kid was back on the stool and speaking to Josh. "It was me. I did it. And for no reason at all." He slapped Josh on the back, a friendly little smack as if they were players on the same football team and Josh had just done something that moved the ball toward the goal. "Hell, I didn't even know whose house that was. I don't even know anybody who lives on Sixth Street."

No, not the piano. A harp. The curly headed brother played the harp and they called him Harpo. Of course.

"I had these sandwiches, see," the kid continued, "and I didn't want them, so I just turned in a driveway—random-like, you know?—tossed them up on the porch and took off." He paused a moment and looked thoughtful. "Must have been some kind of impulse."

Harpo Marx. That was it. The Marx Brothers. Josh would come home way past his curfew and instead of yelling, his dad would be sitting in the dark watching old movies and say, "You gotta see this one, kiddo. This is a classic, and it is part of my sacred duty as your father to educate you as regards slapstick." Josh would drop down on the couch next to his father and watch the movie, or rather, watch his father watch the movie, enjoying his laughter. In the dark room, the images from the TV would flash and shine on his father's face which was, by then, a serious shade of yellow.

"Yeah, officer, you got me. I confess," the kid was saying in a high squeaky voice. "It was me that did it. But officer, I didn't mean to throw those sandwiches on that nice old lady's porch. I was responding to—what do they call it? An irresistible impulse. That's it. Mr. Judge, your honor, have mercy, please. I'm a victim of an irresistible impulse."

Josh looked at the kid again and except for his curly hair, he looked nothing like Harpo Marx.

"Man, I didn't expect to make the paper though. Right there on page three. That was a bonus. Great, huh?"

"How did you know it was an old lady's house?"

"What?"

"You said it was a little old lady. If you didn't know whose house it was, how did you know an old lady lived there?"

"Well, I'll tell you—-what'd you say your name was?"

"Josh."

"So here it is, Josh. It's the power of deduction. After the fact, you know, ipso facto. Two things tell me it's a little old lady. One, who else but an old lady would take the time to count the number of sandwiches? And two, who else but an old lady would call the cops to report that there were sandwiches on her porch? And three—okay, so there're three things—and three, there were not thirty-seven grilled cheese sandwiches. There were only seventeen and who else would exaggerate but some little old lady who's got nothing better to do with her time than count the sandwiches on her porch, call the cops, and then lie about it?"

"Where'd you get the sandwiches?"

"What?" The kid looked incredulous that Josh would have any further questions.

"I mean, what were you doing with all those sandwiches? Where did you get them? I'm just curious."

"Jeez, Josh. You can ask. You can ask all you want." The kid stood up. His voice boomed. "But I ain't telling. Hell, I don't know you well enough yet to go into *that*. That—" He spread his arms wide as if he were a preacher gesturing to a crowd of disciples right there in the K & L Donut Shop. "That, my man, is a whole 'nother story." He laughed, nodded his head slightly at Shannon who giggled, and sailed toward the door. "See you around, new guy."

"Yeah, see you in the funny papers." That was something else his dad used to say, though Josh was never sure what it meant.

Once the kid was gone the donut shop seemed smaller and drabber. It was back to being a small storefront, narrow as a two-lane bowling alley, with a few chipped formica-topped tables and chairs. *How this place stays open is anybody's guess,* Josh thought. Although there wasn't a crumb or a coffee ring at the counter where the kid had been seated, Shannon sauntered over and wiped at it anyway.

Josh picked up the newspaper again, intending to look at the help wanted ads but put it down to ask, "Who was that guy?"

"Oh, that's Chance."

What kind of a name is Chance? Sounds like a cowboy. Last chance. Fat chance. Not a chance. Like his dad would say whenever Josh asked to drive his old VW bug. "Not a chance, kiddo." He'd look so solemn, but then he'd wink and smile and hold out the keys. "On second thought… yes."

Josh looked up at Shannon. *She's not bad looking. Big brown eyes and shiny brown hair with bangs cut straight across her forehead.*

"So, what's there to do on a Friday?"

"Look around awhile," his Aunt Tess had said. "Meet some people. Most folks here are pretty friendly."

"Oh, Friday's easy. People from all over to go to the mall. Well, we call it the mall. It's the Rogers Sale really," Shannon laughed. "Not a mall at all. It's outdoors, you know, a really big flea market. They sell chickens and goats and stuff, but all kinds of other stuff too. My dad says that one time this guy showed up at the Rogers Sale with a bunch of emus he wanted to sell. You know what they are, right? Well, a couple of them got loose and ran all over the place. They caught one of them, but the other one never turned up."

Shannon reached under the counter and pulled out a purse covered in yellow sequins the size of quarters. She held it up by its strap for his inspection, and even in the dim light of the donut shop the spangly pieces blinked and sparkled. "I got this there a couple of weeks ago. It was a really good price, you know? Costs maybe three times as much in a department store."

You could hypnotize somebody with that thing, Josh thought, *or trigger a seizure.* Shannon put the purse back under the counter and there was a moment of silence. A flea market didn't sound like anything special to Josh. *Just what kind of town is this?* He hadn't passed any chain restaurants, movie theaters, or shopping centers on his way here. It was beginning to look like working might be the only thing to do.

"Say, do you know of any jobs around here?"

"Well, they're hiring at the Lots & Lots, I know. My cousin Amy just got a job there." Shannon smiled. "Course there's the casino across the river but you gotta be at least twenty-one for those jobs, I think. And then there's the telemarketing place in Wellsville. They are *always* looking for people. Everybody around here has worked there at least once, but nobody stays long cause the pay is awful. I've worked there twice. For a while just before last Christmas when I needed money for school—I'm going to be an interior designer—and then last month for a couple of days. I couldn't stand it though. People think they can say anything to you over the phone. Here at least people have to look you in the eye before they say anything nasty."

Shannon dropped her eyes for a minute, long enough for Josh to remember some of the things he had said to telemarketers when they called his house. He always pictured them as older women. *Losers,* he remembered thinking. *Get a real job.*

"So where is this Lots & Lots?"

"On St. Clair—I guess you're not from here, huh?"

Took her long enough to figure that out, Josh thought, but then he felt bad. *It's not like she's dumb or anything. And when she smiles, she is—*

"Well, you go out here and turn left at the light and that's St. Clair, so just keep on it a ways, just keep going up the hill, past the cemetery and the park and all, and you'll come to Calcutta and then the Lots & Lots is on the right. You can't miss it. It's not far, maybe a couple miles, well, probably more like five." She hooked her hair behind her ear. "No more than six, I guess." *It's a little elfin ear*, Josh noticed. "Guess I'm not so good at figuring distances."

"I'm sure I'll find it. Thanks."

"If you do miss it, if you go too far, you'll end up on the highway and won't be able to get off for miles. But I have no idea how many miles." And here she allowed herself to laugh out loud.

"Sure. Well, thanks again."

Before he left, Shannon offered directions to the Rogers Sale too. "Just in case," she said.

No way, Josh thought.

At the curb, he rolled the Beetle's radio dial past a half dozen country music stations until he heard a Zeppelin tune start its wind up. His father used to blast heavy metal music loud enough for the windows to rattle. Jimmy Page was his all-time favorite. *Classic rock. At least that's something.* Feeling no irresistible urge about either the Lots & Lots or the flea market, Josh gripped the steering wheel for a few minutes and tried to decide what to do next. Or at least on a direction.

"So, kiddo," his dad used to say. "Where did the day take you?"

Up, Josh thought. *From here it's the only real choice.*

Just when he thought he'd need to stop at a gas station to ask for directions, Josh rounded the corner and there it was, the Rogers Sale. He hadn't planned on going there, but his quick stop at the Lots & Lots—which turned out to be a big box store with too much parking lot—had been fruitless. ("Sorry, the manager won't be back until Monday, and no, no one else can take an application.") Rather than go back to his aunt's, Josh had decided to look for the flea market.

"Explore," his aunt had said. "Look around."

When he encountered a long line of cars stopped on the road, the drivers waiting to turn into a massive gravel lot that encompassed a network of long, low buildings, he realized he'd arrived. The area was crowded with vehicles, pedestrians, and spidery rows of tables laden with merchandise. Josh maneuvered the Beetle over bumps and dips in the parking lot and nosed it into a narrow slot between two pick-up trucks. Street fair aromas greeted him before he was out of the car: the hot grease of french fries and something sweet. Cotton candy? Barbecued meat? A man in a faded red *Jesus Got 'Er Done* tee shirt leaned against the tailgate of a Chevy pick-up and nodded solemnly as Josh looked around, deciding where to go next.

If the donut shop was rendered in shades of gray and brown, as quiet and dim as the cave of a hibernating bear, the Rogers Sale resembled Oz at Dorothy's arrival—bright with sunshine and alive with people in brightly colored clothes. Josh wandered, passing through a doorway and into the nearest pavilion which was occupied by stacks of cages holding live chickens. A sign announced a poultry auction at noon. Josh moved through the building and out to a midway through another set of open doors. From there he watched customers select bananas and examine quarts of strawberries at a produce stand. Next to it was a red and white french fry wagon, exactly like ones Josh had seen at street fairs back home in Cleveland. The cook, a woman with a long ponytail, leaned on the counter with her arm and gazed into space. Josh strolled down an aisle, moving his eyes back and forth to scan tables displaying what look like pirated DVDs, cheap sunglasses, Beanie Babies, and religious pamphlets that asked where he would like to spend eternity. He muttered a quick "no thanks" to the man who offered him one. Harley tee shirts, piles of *Country Life* magazines, eight-track tapes—a lot of this stuff looked like garage sale rejects, while others appeared to be bulk-purchased made-in-China junk like pink plastic back scratchers and bags of tube socks.

Following one aisle led him to another pavilion, this one dominated by a deli counter under a banner that read *Amish Chees-*

es. Aproned young women, their hair tucked under white caps, passed small plastic bags down to shoppers.

"Slice it really thin," a woman next to Josh said to one of the girls. "As thin as you can make it without it crumbling. Got that? Really, really thin. And then I want a quarter pound of the—."

Past the deli, Josh noticed a blonde woman in a wheelchair. A little girl, five or six maybe, was sitting on her lap and pleading, "Please, Mommy, please. I'll take care of it." Are they selling puppies here? Kittens? But as he came closer, he saw that the mother and child were peering into a shallow metal pan on the table, and in the pan were tiny live turtles, the backs of which have been crudely painted with happy faces, rainbows, or butterflies.

"I want a rainbow one, Mommy," the little girl said while holding her mother's face in both her small hands. The mother smiled and laughed, but instead of saying yes or no, she handed her daughter some money. The little girl passed the money on to the woman behind the table.

"Five dollars more, honey, and you get this little pond with a palm tree, a home for your little guy. Would you like that too, honey?" the turtle lady said, smiling like she's made the sale of the century. The girl hugged her mother, one of those fierce, smothering hugs that only little kids can give. At that moment, watching them, listening to the mother ask the question that parents of small children constantly pose ("What do you say to the nice lady?"), Josh realized that he had not thought of his dad for the last hour.

"You're too young to be on your own," his aunt had said when she'd come to Cleveland to help him pack his stuff and move him down to her place. His father had been dead a few weeks by then. "Seventeen is far too young, so you're coming home with me and that's all there is to it. But let me tell you, Joshua Russell. You get in trouble down there and they will not care that you are just seventeen. They will throw the book at you. They will," she said, her expression serious, "put you under the jail."

"Beep!" Someone behind him shouted and Josh jumped. It was Chance, the kid from the donut shop. He was on a mo-

66

torized cart, the kind they advertise on TV for old people to get around in.

"Is that yours?" Josh wondered if this guy had some kind of disability.

"Fancy meeting you here," Chance said. He was all smiles and twinkles, perched on the scooter's seat and beaming. *He looks like a bear on a tricycle,* Josh thought, *but from his expression you'd think he was tooling through town in a Porsche.*

"Naw, I'm just helping a buddy out. He rents them out by the hour here so people will try them and maybe buy one. I'm just riding around to stir up interest. Marketing, you know. So, what're you looking at?" He scooted closer to the table. "You in the market for a turtle?"

Josh turned back to the turtle lady. He'd been wondering about something. "Can't you get some kind of disease from those?"

"Oh, no, not this kind of turtle," the woman replied. "No, no, these are all safe."

"But I read somewhere that you could get something from turtles. Salmonella, was that it? Is that true?"

"No, not at all." The woman continued to smile at him. "These are perfectly safe. No diseases at all."

"Hey! Hey you!" A red-faced man rushed up to them shouting. "Who do you think you are, you son of a bitch?" He reached for Chance, but Chance jumped off the scooter, pulled at Josh's sleeve and shouted, "Let's go." The two of them broke into a run and before he thought about it, Josh took the lead and headed to his car.

"You need a ride?" Josh asked.

"Yeah, I guess I do." Chance was panting and shaking his head. "Guess the boss forget to tell that guy I was marketing today. Some kind of miscommunication apparently." He was still laughing as he got into Josh's car.

"Meet some people," his aunt had said.

*   *   *

"Stop the car a minute. I want to show you something," said Chance. He'd directed Josh to take an exit from the flea market that looked nothing like the road he'd come in on. After a few turns that confused Josh even further, they were on a narrow, rutted road with a cornfield on one side and an expanse of low rough grass on the other.

"Don't worry, nobody's coming. Just stop here a minute," Chance said. At his urging, Josh got out and came around to the front of the car, where Chance was waiting for him.

"Okay, ready? Look at this." Chance pulled a handful of brightly painted turtles out of his pants pocket. "What do you think, huh?"

"You stole those? While I was talking to that lady, you stole some of her turtles?"

"Sure did." Chance flashed his merry prankster grin. Most of the turtles were on their backs, legs pedaling, necks craning. One had a blue peace sign painted on its shell.

"So, here's what we're gonna do," Chance said. "I'm going to put the turtles in front of your wheel and then you're going to drive over them. You have to do it really slow though because I want to video this whole thing on my phone. I figure if you do it slow, their shells will crunch loud enough to hear on the video."

Josh felt sick. *He didn't just say that.*

"What are you talking about? Why would you do that?"

Instead of answering him, Chance dropped turtles one by one in front of Josh's left front tire.

"No! This is crazy!" Josh shouted. "No!" Chance had his cell phone out, ready to record. "No! I'm not doing this!"

Without missing a beat, Chance pocketed his phone and said, "Suit yourself." Before Josh could move, before he could kneel down to pick up the turtles, Chance stomped on one, and then another, and then another, grinding each with the heel of his shoe.

"Stop it, God damn you." Josh stepped forward and what happened next, happened fast. It ended quickly too, with Chance on the ground, wiping blood from his mouth with the back of his sleeve. Josh got in his car and backed up so he could drive around Chance and the gore on the ground.

As he pulled away, Chance shouted, "Don't worry, new guy. I'll hitch a ride."

"Meet some people," his aunt had said.

Minutes later, Josh realized he was lost. He'd turned off the rutted road and onto something a little wider that seemed more promising, but he couldn't find the highway or any indication that he was headed back into East Liverpool. From the opposite direction, a red Ford Focus came towards him, and Josh thought he'd ask the driver for directions. But the Ford stopped about thirty feet in front of him. Had it stalled out? He slowed, intending to stop when he got next to the Ford so he could talk to the driver, a blonde-haired woman.

Josh suddenly realized the driver's attention was focused on the cornfield to his right. He turned to look. Tentatively, gingerly, in a single file, six deer stepped from the field and walked as if on tiptoe out onto the pavement. They were so close to him—only three or four feet away—that Josh could see their ears flicker, could almost measure the long lashes on their immense eyes. Their hair glistened as their muscles rippled beneath the skin. On spindly legs, each deer crossed the road between the two cars, then deftly leapt over the culvert, dashed across the grassy strip in front of a copse of oaks and maples, and was gone.

"Oh my gosh," Josh said aloud. Although the last deer had disappeared, he couldn't move his foot from the brake to the gas pedal.

Slowly, the woman in the red car drove forward. When she was alongside Josh, she nodded and smiled.

"So, what do you think?" Tess asked him, when he strolled through the back door. She was standing at the kitchen counter assembling a salad. "Did you get a good look around?"

"Yeah, I drove around awhile. Ended up at that big outdoor sale at—where is it?—Rogers?"

"Oh, Jeez," Tess laughed. "This is Friday, isn't it? Bet it was packed."

"It seemed crowded, yeah." And then, as if one thought logically led to the other, he added, "Think I'm going to get a job. Somebody said they're hiring at that Lots & Lots store."

Knife poised over a tomato, Tess stopped and cocked her head in his direction. "You like tomatoes on your salad?" He nodded and she began slicing. "A job would be good. Be a good way to meet people and get settled in."

Josh thought about going to his room to listen to some music, but he didn't want to be rude. They'd driven south in their separate cars last night, stopping for dinner on their way only after they were out of Cuyahoga County, but they'd both been quiet. In the morning he'd slept late, and then had only seen his aunt for a few minutes before she left for work.

"I hope you'll give people a chance, Josh," Tess said. "I know it's been difficult with your dad's death and all, but this, moving here, this could be a new start for you. You could rest here. No, I don't mean rest." She frowned. "I don't mean that you're tired, physically tired, I just mean… look." She scooped sliced tomatoes into her hands and dropped them onto the greens that already filled a large bowl, a salad mammoth enough to feed far more than just the two of them. She wiped her hands on a dish towel and turned to him.

"Josh, I'm not good at talking about things, I guess, but I just want to say that I hope you'll give this a chance. If we can both be positive about it, see it as the start of new possibilities…. Well, it'll be better than if we don't." The look on her face told him she wasn't satisfied with what she was saying or how she was saying it. "Do you see what I'm trying to say?"

He wished she'd stopped talking. *What good are words? They never fix anything.* Ever since his dad died, everybody talked at him, asking about his feelings and what he'd like to do, where he'd like to live, as if he had any say in the matter. His dad was never like this. The two of them never had to stand around talking and talking.

70

Josh sat down at the little oak table in Tess' bright, cheery kitchen and noticed that since this morning she had moved a stack of books and papers off the table to make room for him. He watched as she added diced chicken to the salad and topped it with croutons.

"You want to find us something to watch on TV," his aunt asked. "I thought we'd eat in the front room where it's cooler."

Josh walked into the living room. He found the remote and punched the TV on. The television flashed instantly to life, and there was Humphrey Bogart, tugging at the rim of his fedora and muttering something to a woman, a brunette with dreamy, half-closed eyes. His dad would have called her a babe. He looked from the TV to the doorway where his aunt was standing, holding a tray with their dinner.

"You like old movies?" his aunt asked. "You know who that is?"

"Of course. It's Bogie," Josh laughed. "He's the best."

Tess put the tray down on the coffee table, started for the kitchen and then stopped.

"Help me out here, Josh. I don't know what you like yet. You want milk, or a soda, or iced tea with this?"

"Iced tea would be great," Josh said.

On the TV Bogie smiled slyly at the babe.

FIRST STONE

Gilbert Grum sat at the kitchen table and scanned *The Morning Herald.* He nodded his agreement to the editorial opposing the East Liverpool school levy and smiled at the strange behaviors of his fellow citizens as noted in the police blotter. All the while he listened for the first stirrings of Cheryl.

Gilbert gave every appearance of a man relaxed. An hour ago, he had been anything but that was when the morning sun poked through the gap in the bedroom curtains, jolting him awake and delivering a certainty that he was going to be late for work. But when he turned and looked, first at Cheryl—only a mound under the floral comforter with a swirl of blonde curls trailing out—and then at the alarm clock, he remembered that his life had changed. He was a free man. After thirty-six years of service to Phoenix Pottery, he had retired. His second thought: *I'm at risk of sleeping away the first day of my new life, one in which I can do whatever I want.*

So here he was, up and ready to go, quietly enjoying the newspaper and a second cup of coffee. A curious police blotter blurb caught his attention. Cecil Somebody had been hauled off for what sounded like a psychiatric evaluation when, during a "heated verbal dispute" with his sixty-four-year-old girlfriend, he had threatened to harm himself with a potato peeler. The event sounded like so many others that made the paper: crazy antics fueled, no doubt, by drugs and/or alcohol and/or desperation. But the name Cecil made this one noteworthy. Such an old-fashioned name, unusual these days. Hadn't Gilbert known a guy named Cecil? Surely not, but wait—*Wait.*

72

Cecil Coathanger. Of course.

When Gilbert was four or five he had an imaginary friend named Cecil Coathanger. His mother would lock the door when he went outside to play so he couldn't come in and untidy her scrupulously tidy house. When he had to go to the bathroom, he'd knock and knock on the door, but she couldn't hear him over the vacuum, so he'd go to the neighbor's house, a practice that had probably not made his mother popular. One day the neighbor lady was out, so Gilbert pooped on the seat of his tricycle. He wished he could remember how he had come to make that choice, to use his tricycle for a toilet instead of, say, choosing anyplace in their fairly private backyard. He recalled that the sight of a little mound of something that had come out of his body had frightened him. He was about to poke it with a stick when his mother emerged from the house, and that's when he realized there was something more alarming than the poo—the look on his mother's face. In his panic, he blurted out that the deed had been done by Cecil Coathanger.

The incident became a story his mother told for the next several decades. He remembered a 4th of July cookout during his teens when he was standing around the grill with his dad and uncles. His dad said, "Hey, Buddy, go ask your mom if she wants these burgers well done or what." When Gilbert slipped into the kitchen, dense with women smoking or fussing over the potato salad, they turned to him and laughed. "How is your friend Cecil doing, sweetheart?" one of his aunts asked, and the women threw their heads back and laughed even more. His mother lived to be ninety-two and while her memory slipped a gear or two those last years, she never forgot the tricycle incident. The older she got, the less the story was about a small boy's charmingly childish attempt to shift blame to the little man who wasn't there and the more she embellished the fecal aspect of the story, wondering aloud how he had managed to balance it so perfectly on the bike seat. And it didn't stop even after she'd gone to the nursing home. He walked into her room once as she was regaling a young aide with the story, going so far as to claim that he'd styled it like a Dairy Queen cone with a curl on top. Adult Gilbert simply stood there, waiting for the giggling to stop so he could ask if the aide had any idea where all his mother's nightgowns had gone.

Enough of that. Mother is gone now. Gilbert's thoughts shifted back to his retirement, specifically on the careful financial planning that enabled it. Even though Cheryl had retired at sixty-two from her job as a 911 dispatcher a couple of years before, they were, as far as Gilbert could tell, set. Sacrifices had been made, of course. Gilbert had taken as much overtime as he could get, and they had scrounged, eliminating vacations for the last few years, downsizing Christmas, birthday and anniversary celebrations. Did they really need to go out for a movie? And how had the Friday fish fries at the American Legion become such a habit? Gilbert had trained himself to cut back on even the smallest of luxuries, like gum and candy bars. As a result, with their pensions, Social Security, IRAs, and a savings account elevated last year by a small inheritance from the last of Gilbert's aunts (*It was the least she could do*, he now thought), he was relatively certain they could get by in at least some degree of comfort.

"It's about time, Sleepyhead," Gilbert said as Cheryl stepped into the kitchen. Anyone else would look disheveled at this point in the morning, but not Cheryl. The curls had been tamed and she was dressed for the day in blue knit pants and a tee shirt that featured large sunflowers. Not a yawn betrayed her.

"Coffee's ready, and I can pop a bagel in the toaster for you." Cheryl had made his breakfast for decades, so wasn't it time he returned the favor?

Cheryl nodded and took a long look out the window to the backyard where a half dozen peonies drooped, their pink blossoms nearly touching the ground. Nearby, a trio of gold finches jostled each other at the feeder, all twitters and flutters of yellow wings.

"What would you like to do today?" Gilbert asked. He grinned as he spread just a dab of safe-for-your-heart margarine on the last raisin bagel.

"What?"

"I just happen to be free all day, remember? We could spend it together. You want to go somewhere? Do something?"

"You can do whatever you like, Gilbert, but I've got this house to clean, and then I'll be gone all afternoon. Don't worry. I'll be home in time to make your dinner."

Ah, yes, it's Monday. What does she do on Mondays? Tuesdays she volunteers at the historical society and Thursdays are something at the library, isn't it? But what's on Mondays?

"I wasn't worried about dinner. I thought we ought to do something special since it's the first day of my retirement. Kinda try it out, you know?"

"You know good and well I've got bowling. I'd never be able to get a sub this late, and besides, we're in second place. They need me."

Ah yes, bowling—an activity, a habit, that Gilbert had not been able to convince Cheryl to forego. He did recall hearing something about the recent triumphs of the Monday league. And Cheryl spoke often of one particular friend on her team. *Trissy? or Chrissy? Maybe Prissy? No, that couldn't be right.* He mentally shrugged and turned back to the paper. Well, he could certainly find something to do. Something spontaneous. That was the beauty of retirement. You could wake up in the morning and act on the first impulse that arose. Gone were the days when he'd be at the pottery all day, putting ears on stacks of cups for hours, or training a new employee, or trying to figure out why there was so much breakage in the new color. He could have told them Riotous Raspberry would be trouble, but they wouldn't have listened. They never did. He sighed. *Well, it's not my problem anymore.*

Gilbert found a schedule of local events in the paper, skimmed through the listings, and waited for an impulse. Here was something: a nature walk this very afternoon in Beaver Creek State Park with a guide who would point out edible mushrooms. Now, this was exactly the sort of thing he'd always wanted to do. He could imagine himself coming home with a bucket of pale, delicate mushrooms and presenting them to Cheryl. "Grill these with the steaks, dear," he would tell her. Oh, but they'd eliminated steak some time ago. Well, perhaps this particular nature walk wasn't the one for him, but something along those lines would be interesting. Something educational and out of doors. Birds maybe. Or bugs. He'd been fascinated by bugs when he was a boy. He used to bring all kinds of many-legged beasties home and his mother, boy, she would pitch a fit. Claimed she could hear them, bent on escape and a dash to freedom, their tiny legs scritch-scratching against the sides of an empty coffee can.

Her breakfast finished, Cheryl stood in the kitchen spraying cleaner on the counter and vigorously wiping it down.

"How about I run the vacuum?" Gilbert looked around as if the vacuum would materialize simply because he was thinking about it. *Cheryl keeps it somewhere…a closet maybe? But which one?*

"Don't be silly. I've got it down to a system. It doesn't take me any time at all."

Okay, I'll take a walk then. Gilbert folded the paper back into its original form. Cheryl hadn't seen it yet, and she appreciated a tidy newspaper. At least he did, and he supposed she did too. He stood and stretched and tried not to give in to the yawn he felt creep across his body. *Gentleman of leisure I might be, but I'm not about to begin my retirement with a nap.*

"A morning walk might be a good habit for me to get into, don't you think?" But Cheryl was damp-mopping the kitchen floor and only nodded when he said goodbye.

Outside, Gilbert paused to examine the front of his home. A tidy two-bedroom brick ranch, he and Cheryl had lived here since the third year of their marriage, thinking they'd move on depending on how big the family grew. But children never arrived, a subject that still saddened Gilbert. Cheryl said it just wasn't meant to be and they should make the best of it. So, they never left their brick home on Claire Lane, but steadily paid the mortgage down and improved it bit by bit, installing new windows and adding a wooden deck. They owned it free and clear now, a goal achieved.

76

"Free and clear," Gilbert said aloud, thinking of the new roof he'd put on with some buddies just last summer, back when he was still prefacing all his thoughts for the future with a list of tasks to accomplish before his retirement.

Maybe I'll start walking tomorrow, Gilbert decided. Today he'd drive around to see what the wider world had on offer. Once out of the driveway, he found himself headed for the business district. *I am definitely not going to Burger Meister. No sir.* Before he had decided to cut back on such frivolous expenditures, he'd run in there once in a while for a sandwich and there'd they be, the old guys, sitting around one of the big round tables, holding court, crabbing about everything wrong with the world. Not exactly exalted knights of the Round Table, Gilbert had thought. A couple of them had worked at the pottery. They'd wave and invite him over, but he always said, "Sorry. Things to do."

Dave Rivers was one of them. He was much older than Gilbert, of course. He had, in fact, trained Gilbert years ago. Some of the other guys used to rib Dave about how long he'd worked at the pottery. "You've been around since the Indians used to run through here stealing the light bulbs, ain't that right?" Craig What's-His-Name used to say that. Craig was one of those guys who had about three interesting things to say and repeated them endlessly.

Gilbert used to wonder what kind of Indians, which tribe? Indians had once lived here, he knew that. He'd seen the arrowhead collection somebody had donated to the Wellsville River Museum. All locally found, the little card next to the display said.

Hey, maybe I'll take that up as a hobby, collecting arrowheads.

As he drove past Burger Meister, Gilbert wondered if there were still arrowheads out there waiting to be found. Or was he too late? Say, maybe he should invest in one of those metal detectors he'd once seen a guy with at the park, swinging it slowly back and forth across a small patch of grass. That could be an interesting hobby. Not that he'd find arrowheads that way, of course, but who knew what he could turn up?

When Gilbert and Cheryl bought their home, cornfields dominated the nearby countryside. Over the years those had been transformed into strip malls and shops. The hardware store where Gilbert had bought his lawnmower was there, as was Lots & Lots, a twenty-four-hour mega store with groceries at one end and on the other—seemingly a half mile away—everything else families could possibly need. Cheryl shopped for their groceries there once a week, but Gilbert now realized he could take over that task. And why not? He could lighten her load. It was only fair. Cheryl had done all the housework, prepared all the meals while he'd only taken care of the lawn. *Well, I plow the drive and shovel the sidewalk when it snows, so there's that too.*

Like toys spread across a playroom, shopping carts were scattered helter-skelter across the parking area of the Lots & Lots. Gilbert pushed the first one he came to, aimed it into the second cart he saw, and so on, building a train of carts that, as it grew, became increasingly unwieldy. A blonde young man in the emerald green shirt of a Lots & Lots employee approached him, smiling shyly.

"Thanks a lot, sir. I can take these now," the boy said, reaching for the carts.

"No problem. I'm going in myself so I might as well take these with me."

"No, that's okay. I'll take them from here. Thanks though." Again, the boy reached for the carts.

Gilbert tightened his grip on the cart's handle. He nodded to his left. "Why don't you get those at the far end, and I'll just push these in?"

"Um, I'm supposed to be doing this. I mean, they pay me to do this."

Gilbert squinted at the name tag on the kid's shirt. "Look, Josh, I don't mind. I've got them this far so I may as well finish the job." He leaned into his heavy cargo, straining to get the carts closer to the door. The young man shrugged and walked away.

A slight rise in the pavement just before the automatic doors caused Gilbert to grit his teeth and bear down harder. Inside, he struggled to align the carts with a row that was already there. A middle-aged man in a green jacket and tie emerged from the corner office, just as Gilbert realized that Josh was behind him with more carts.

"Thanks again, sir," Josh said. Gilbert liked that "sir" business—unusual from such a young fellow these days—and nodded his approval.

"Hey you!" Someone shouted. Gilbert turned but the man wasn't looking at him so he walked further into the store. "Yeah, you, new kid. Didn't I tell you to get those carts?"

Gilbert found himself standing in the produce section, wondering where he might find the raisin bagels. Above him, a sign hanging from the ceiling featured a cartoon figure of a man wearing a polka dot tie and an over-sized baseball cap. LUCKY LARRY SEZ SAVING IS FUN! the sign proclaimed in neon orange and green letters. *Not the sort of colors the pottery would want to try. And there's something odd about that facial expression. It's what Dad used to call a shit-eating grin.*

In front of him, a hand-lettered sign over a mound of lettuce announced "Today's Super Special Value" at fifty-nine cents a head. Cheryl was always running out of lettuce. He should pick up a few heads. Gilbert selected one and then another. With one in each hand he considered the heft of each. He spotted a produce scale hanging about a dozen feet away. Gilbert determined that the first head of lettuce was two ounces heavier than the second. *Okay, that one.* He went back to the lettuce display, picked out another head and weighed it. It too was heavier than the second one he'd chosen. *Okay, I'll take that one too.* After a few minutes of weighing and contemplating, Gilbert ended up with four satisfactorily heavy heads of lettuce in his arms. *Should have grabbed a cart,* he thought, but he hadn't actually planned on shopping. Pleased, he realized that this too was a retirement benefit he could enjoy. You could shop at your leisure and take advantage of bargains whenever you found them. As he stood there cradling the heads of lettuce, a young woman in a grey business suit approached, her high heels clicking on the tile floor.

"You can weigh those over there, you know," Gilbert said.

The woman looked puzzled.

"If you weigh them," Gilbert nodded toward the scale, "you can find the heaviest and buy it. It's a better buy."

"What?"

"They're priced per head, see. So, if you buy the heaviest one, you get more for your money."

The young woman chewed her lower lip, looked away, then continued sorting through the heads. Gilbert stepped closer.

"They don't all weigh the same, see, but they cost the same, so if you…"

"I don't want any lettuce," the woman said and walked away. As the percussion of her heels faded, Gilbert marveled at the notion of anyone willingly ignoring an opportunity to save money.

After he picked up a bag of Cheryl's favorite bagels and added it to the quartet of lettuce heads he still hugged to his chest, Gilbert meandered through the non-edible side of Lots & Lots. Here too Lucky Larry reigned supreme, leering at shoppers from ceiling-hung signs that swayed ever so slightly. In the sporting goods department—where Larry wore a green bowler hat and rather angrily, Gilbert thought, shook a fistful of shamrocks—Gilbert considered again the possibilities of a hobby. Juggling his purchases, he reached out to smooth his fingers across the fabric of a tent that was on display. Camping. He'd been a Boy Scout briefly, he remembered, until his mother said she didn't have time to take him to and from all those meetings. He tried to imagine Cheryl enjoying a night or two sleeping under the stars. Did he really want to learn how to erect one of these tents? An RV might be a better idea. Yes, they could drive to Yellowstone, the Grand Canyon, Mount Rushmore maybe, and sleep in their own bed every night right next to a tidy little kitchen. That he could picture: Cheryl taking one of her special lasagnas from a tiny oven and serving it to him on a tiny table. RVs were expensive. But wait—if they sold the house, they could wander across America, heading south in the winter, staying at camp-grounds. Or friend's driveways. He could bring his metal detector. It would be a different kind of life, one full of adventure. Befriending strangers at various campgrounds. Meeting folksy old men who ran the little groceries. Doing their laundry at the local laundromat. He tried to imagine Cheryl in a laundromat. *Well, maybe not.*

Lazily fluttering above him, Lucky Larry wore a Hawaiian shirt and sported an orange mullet.

"Stop smashing into me," someone shouted, and Gilbert noticed two kids in the checkout line next to his. The boy wore a Pittsburgh Steeler's baseball cap. The girl, who couldn't be more than six or seven, had brown pigtails and a purple ruffly dress. A thought raced through Gilbert's mind: *Cheryl and I might have had grandchildren about this age.* The little girl twirled her dress while she twisted back and forth and hung on to the arm of a thin, tired-looking woman in a pink tee shirt. Gilbert looked closer at the mother. *She's one of those skinny, wired-up women, and as jumpy as a tick, by the look of her.*

"Get off me," the mother said, shaking the girl off her arm. And then, in one fluid motion, the mother picked up a candy bar from the display next to her elbow and tossed it into a purse in her cart.

Marketing, Gilbert thought. *The people who run these stores are clever and put things they think you'll buy on an impulse close to the cashier, so while you're waiting, you'll pick up something you hadn't planned on buying, like gum. Or those stupid tabloid magazines.* Most people were susceptible to this sort of thing, buying things they didn't need without thinking, but Gilbert had trained himself not to give in those little temptations.

Wait.

Did that woman just steal a candy bar? And right in front of her kids?

"How was school today?" The mother asked the little girl who began a jittery little dance and launched into a story about a spelling test. "I got all of them right, Mommy. Every single word."

"That's good, honey."

I bet she's done this before, Gilbert thought. He stared at her. You could never tell what's going on inside a person. Cheryl often said that, a statement often accompanied with a shake of her head and a sad look of resignation. She was right. You just never knew about people, what they got up to when no one was looking. Or when they thought no one was looking.

Gilbert continued to stare at the woman, hoping she'd become aware of his doing so. And then what? Would he say something?

Now the boy was telling the woman about his day at school, something about his homework. Gilbert wasn't eavesdropping, not really, but he wanted to hear if this woman would tell the cashier about the candy bar. He wanted to hear her say, "Oh, and ring this up for me too."

She didn't.

When it was Gilbert's turn to check out, he thought he might say something to his cashier. He began to frame words in his head (*I think I saw that woman....*), but the cashier was like some of the teenagers he'd noticed lately, a sour looking girl with a sullen look. "So what," she'd probably say. Maybe she'd tell him to mind his own business the way Cheryl sometimes—

"Thank you for shopping at Lots & Lots," the cashier droned in his general direction. *I remember when they used to count out the change. And look at you. They used to look at you. And smile. They used to smile and count your change right into your hand.* That Josh fellow had smiled at him and called him "sir." *At least the store's got one decent employee.*

He could tell the manager about the candy bar. But there, in the doorway he hesitated which caused another customer to bump into him. *Forget it,* he thought. *None of your business, as Cheryl would say if she were here.*

Once outside, Gilbert saw the woman loading her groceries into an ancient minivan, rust creeping around its doors. He got into his pickup. *Where does somebody like this live, somebody who would do such a thing right in front of her own children?* He followed her down St. Clair, made a right turn at Woodland and another at Avondale where the minivan pulled into a drive next to a two-story house.

From his spot at the curb, Gilbert noted that the lawn could use a trim and the roof wouldn't last another year. He could count the sprung shingles. He watched as the children carried groceries into the house and heard the screen door bang behind them. The woman, a couple of plastic Lots & Lots bags in one hand and a gallon of milk in the other, started towards the door. And then she stopped. She turned, slowly, and looked at Gilbert.

Her expression wasn't puzzled, or angry, or hostile like the cashier's. She looked afraid. *Is she afraid of me? When in my life have I ever frightened anyone? Maybe I should go talk to her, tell her that even if she had taken that candy bar—wait. Did I really see that? Did I hear everything she said to the cashier? Can I be sure? And even if she had taken it, it was just a stupid candy bar. Maybe she's a single mom doing her best with those kids and oh, here's an idea. If she needs help with that roof, I can do that. Maybe my buddies and I can re-shingle her roof just like we did mine.* All that joking and laughter, honest work performed under a hot sun. It had been hard work, he remembered, but it had also been a lot of fun. This woman could bring them tall glasses of lemonade and thank them and they'd say, "Hey, no big deal. What are neighbors for?"

Looking up, Gilbert could see the woman standing in her living room, gazing out the window at him, a telephone in her hand. *Maybe this woman is overwhelmed, maybe she's got a sick father to look after as well as those kids, maybe she's working two jobs just to put food on the table. Okay, so Mom wouldn't take me to scout meetings, but, by golly, she made sure I got to Sunday school every week.* Some of that came back to him now. *Yes, Jesus or Paul or one of those guys said people should carry each other's burdens. "Do unto others." Yes, that's it: "Do unto others." It was a rule.* He thought about all the time he had on his hands now and that nothing, nothing at all came to mind when he considered what he might do with it. *I should knock on her door and introduce myself.* Gilbert reached for the truck's door handle. But when he heard the sirens, when the first police car pulled in front of him and another behind him and a third made a dramatic made-for-TV brake-slamming, tire-squealing stop in the middle of the street, when a policeman put his head into the truck, his angry face inches from Gilbert's and demanded to know why he'd been looking in a little girl's bedroom, Gilbert's thoughts turned to Cheryl.

What am I gonna say to Cheryl?

The Cleaning Fairy's Daughter

I was in the kitchen, aproned, and thinking about biscuits when Melody approached me. The perpetually perky Melody. Calls herself The Hostess, as if Carla's Country Kitchen is some Michelin-starred bistro and not a pretty basic french-fries-on-the-salad West Virginia eatery. For someone who's full of pretensions, Melody is surprisingly well informed on less cultured phenomena like *The Morning Herald*'s police blotter and all the local gossip. She is always and forever minding other people's business and cheerful about all of it, whether it's the death of one of our regulars (like Pete the other week, a rumored suicide) or something Charlie Brown said to Lucy in the comics.

Melody. Such an inappropriate name, I think, as she screeches, "Good morning, Katie. What a shock that must have been, seeing that article in the paper this morning."

Nothing at all melodic about her—not her off-kilter personality, her hoot owl voice, or the weird way she dresses. Six o'clock in the damn morning and she is wearing what seems to be her favorite hostess outfit: an olive-green polyester dress she must have bought during bag day at the Goodwill, open-toed black leather pumps, and huge faux pearl earrings firmly attached to her I-hear-everything ears. She looks like she's ready to interview for a bank teller's position in 1967.

At that moment I think, *What article?* but I will not ask. Melody is being deliberately cryptic, one of her most annoying habits. Her little riddles always turn out to be complete crap, and today I am unwilling to play the game.

So, I wait. She says nothing. The air between us thickens a bit, like the first stage of the white sauce I make for "Carla's Famous Mac & Cheese," a Tri-State Favorite, or so the menu claims. Marlboros are a tri-state favorite too, along with warm Budweiser and two-liter bottles of Diet Pepsi. There is, around here, absolutely no accounting for taste.

And still it goes on, the silence. We are waiting each other out, and a quick look at her tells me that if I can just hold out a tad bit longer, her smile might snap in two. Revealing what, though? I shudder to think.

"Well, you saw it, didn't you?" she asks, finally.

I turn my back to her and pretend to clean the already clean-as-it's-ever-gonna-get griddle. But then, without thinking, I ask:

"Saw what?"

"The article in *The Herald,* the survey results. About your mom."

And there it is. My mother. Again. Just that quickly, the fun I've been having dueling with Melody evaporates as quickly as water on a hot grill.

"Nope. Haven't seen it," I tell her. Big mistake. I have just granted her license to tell me all about it. And she does.

"It's a survey. They have them almost every day but this one was about your mom. The question was 'Would you like a visit from the Cleaning Fairy?' Twenty-two percent of the people who responded said they would like her to come to their house, but seventy-eight percent said no, it would just be" —and here she slows down for emphasis—"too weird."

All at once the kitchen is too small, too hot, and I have to leave. Now. I mumble something about buttermilk for the biscuits, grab my purse, and head for the back door. Once I'm in my car, I decide to sit for however long it takes me to breathe again, but I glance back at the door and there stands Melody, staring out at me, her mouth a gaping maw. I've read that phrase "gaping maw" in a couple of books, and it comes to mind now as I look at her.

With that phrase I picture the mouth of a cave, a cave full of dirt and stink and rotted flesh on old bones. And then I imagine Melody's mouth full of broken yellow teeth and blackened gums. Her mouth does not look like this, you understand, but I see it this way, almost as if she were Dorian Gray in that part of the book when the jig is up and all the ugliness, all that has corrupted his intensely corruptible soul has moved from the canvas he stashed in the attic and taken up residence on his face. I sit there, trying to calm my breathing, and then I pull my car out onto the street.

You probably know about my mother, read about her in the paper or heard the jokes about her on local radio, but in case you missed it, here it is: Lorraine Wheeler, age fifty-seven, former owner of the Pretty Neat Cleaning Service is the Cleaning Fairy of East Liverpool, Ohio. It is not a title she conferred upon herself, you understand. It was a gift from Lewis Witt of *The Morning Herald*. He dubbed her that in the article he wrote when she was arrested for burglary in the home of Sarah and Jon Zellers. Apparently, my mom broke into their house, a charming split level on a dead-end street, and cleaned it. I say "apparently" because to this day my mother has not said a word to me about this little incident. She acknowledges it only as "Oh, that." So my knowledge of the event is limited to whatever Melody, in her selfless generosity, feels like sharing.

According to both Lewis and Melody, once my mother entered the house she washed a few dishes, and then dusted and vacuumed the living room. Oh, and she took out the garbage, cleaned out the cat box, started a load of mixed colors, and scribbled a bill for $65 onto a napkin. She thoughtfully included her phone number and address on the bill, just in case, you know, that they might want to hire/not hire her again.

As reported by Lewis Witt, my mother showed no signs of mental illness when the police picked her up. *Thanks, Lewis. How's* your *mother, by the way?*

This could all be charming in some daffy kind of way. If this were England my mother might be regarded as a colorful eccentric, the kind of person who makes village life, well, entertaining. It might even be regarded as nuttily charming here if she hadn't done this a time or two already. But she has done it at least twice before, and I fear that she is wearing the cops the hell out. After the first arrest a couple of months ago, the judge patiently listened while she explained that she had no idea what had gotten into her and promised to never do it again. He seemed to accept her apparent show of remorse and waved her away. The folks with the need for a clean house in that first instance did not want to appear in court and did not want to talk to the media (aka Lewis).

But a few weeks later it happened again. I shouldn't say "happened" as if it were a lightning strike or an act of God. My mother deliberately entered a locked house (via the window she smashed) where she reportedly straightened the clutter in the family room, scrubbed both bathrooms, and mopped the kitchen floor. She was held overnight this time and though no one says so, it wouldn't have surprised me if she asked for a can of latex so she could spruce the place up a bit.

The judge, on this, the second occasion, admonished her to cut it out. What is it with this judge? Does he think this is funny? I'd have thrown the book at her, but she, no doubt, would have rushed to pick up the damn book, dusted it, and used the Dewey Decimal System to put it in its proper place.

And then last week she did it again. The Zellers were the recipients of her efforts this time, and according to Fred Knight, the attorney I hired, they are less amused than the judge has been. Jon Zellers has a rather extensive and valuable coin collection in the house and although my mother did not steal anything —not a nickel, not a sou, not a euro—the thought that she had the opportunity to do so was enough for the Zellers to press the prosecutor to charge her with everything he could think of.

So here is where we are: three break-ins, three arrests, and two sets of dropped charges and a third set pending. But how did we get here? No doubt it has something to do with her failed business. It's clear that shutting the doors on the Pretty Neat Cleaning

Service—which she had to do last year due to a lack of customers—has left her with entirely too much time on her hands and too much energy in her system.

According to Melody, my mother is "in dire straits and desperate for money." That is not true, not really, but the phrase "dire straits" is a nice touch. Dire Straits was the name of a British rock band, as you probably know, but I think it should be the name of a proudly heterosexual but ironically self-deprecating country band: Charlie Loverboy and the Dire Straights. But hearing the phrase "dire straits" out of Melody's mouth on the day she offered up that tidbit about my mother's motive put me right over the top.

Resplendent in her green polyester dress, the color of that jar of olives that's resided for years way, way back in your fridge, Melody stood there in the middle of Carla's at high noon on a Friday when the place was packed and proceeded to broadcast her theory of the crime for all to hear. Declaiming like a town crier, she announced that my mother, my "poor mother" in her words, had gone round the bend. I could hear her back in the kitchen where I was simultaneously running the grill and making phone calls to arrange mom's bail. This was the morning after the night of her latest arrest. But in the nanosecond between my asking Uncle Lou for the money and the time it took him to say "No, absolutely not," I heard Melody—she who lacks a volume control—say this thing. I hung up the phone, yelled to Randy, our boss, who was back in his office that I was leaving, and I left.

Within the hour, Randy fired me for going AWOL. Later I heard that he got so frazzled trying to fill in for me in the kitchen that he booted everyone out of the place and closed it up, right there and then, in the middle of "Carla's Fabulous Fish Fry, Famous Across the Tri-State Area."

Just for the record I have lived here for all of my thirty-four years and I have never once heard anyone claim that any of the food at Carla's was renowned in this corner of our little West Virginia-Ohio-Pennsylvania triad. In fact, when the restaurant is fairly slow, I amuse myself by mentally amending the menu's claims. For example, instead of bragging that the mac and cheese is a tri-state favorite, the menu should read "Although it is apparently enjoyed by some people, including one or two who may have strayed from over across the river, it is doubtful that people come to West Virginia en masse for the mac and cheese which on a bad day is a tad gummy, if you want to know the truth." *Let's see you fit all that truthfulness on the menu, Randy.*

He hired me back later that same day. If you ask him about it now, Randy would probably deny the incident ever happened. In fact, both of us behaved as though I had never walked out and he had never tried his hand at any of my recipes.

I think about this memory as I drive around a few back streets, killing time before I go back to Carla's. I don't need buttermilk, but I do need time to think. And what I mull over as I drive around is this: Is Melody intentionally malicious or just stupid? The jury is still out on that, and my guess is they will come back deadlocked, unable to reach a verdict because both possibilities are so probable. I'd like to see *The Herald* run a survey on that provocative question.

I end up back in the pockmarked lot at Carla's, where I spend a moment in my car and wonder if I should flatten all of Melody's tires or just two or three. How about the left front and the right rear? I have an affinity for diagonals. The truth is I want to do something, and tire-flattening is the most benign thing that occurs to me. I consider this for a minute or two and then I decide to act.

I'm surprised at how easy it is. I've got my Swiss army knife in my jeans pocket, and it only takes a second for me to realize that the tiny corkscrew is the right tool for the job. Granted, it seems an odd sort of weapon. I could use the tip of one of the knife blades, I suppose, but I've never had a use for the corkscrew before so I'm pleased I can use it now. Besides, there's something amusing about the spiral of the corkscrew that appeals to me. I kneel by Melody's left front tire and let air out of it. As I listen to the satisfying hiss, it occurs to me that tire manufacturers should do something about this. They should invent some kind of lock for the little cap that covers the valve. There are gas cap locks, aren't there? People as annoying, as maddening and judgmental and generally awful as Melody need some kind of security in their lives. And if they've got any self-awareness, such people might be willing to pay a little extra for the assurance that when they come out of work their tires won't be flat.

The hiss of released air seems to go on forever, like the prolonged applause at the end of a really great concert. If, for example, the imaginary Charlie Loverboy and the Dire Straights made it big, they might garner applause as long lasting, as pleasing to the ear as the *pssst* of air escaping Melody's tire. My leg is starting to cramp from the kneeling, so I stand and contemplate my next move. The thought flashes through my mind that I have never, ever done anything like this in my life, and I am thoroughly enjoying it. The tire has a smooshed look, but if I stop now, Melody might think she picked up a nail on her drive into work. Death by natural causes, as it were. And I don't want her to think that. I want her to realize this is some kind of retribution for bad behavior. I want her to understand that karma has come calling.

Letting air out of a second tire goes more quickly. I've got the hang of the process now. As I step back to admire my work, I decide to flatten a third tire because I read in a decorating magazine once that three is an interesting number. Three decorative whatsits on the mantle, three flowerpots on the corner of the patio, three flats on Melody's car. So, I'm kneeling again, this time at the other front tire, when the back door of Carla's flies open and there she stands.

Melody has got her hands on her hips and at first, I take that for anger, an unusual pose for her, uncharacteristically assertive, but the expression on her face says otherwise. In fact, her face reveals nothing. It's as if she has not yet made up her mind how to react to what she's seeing. So, not anger. I would expect anger, would even welcome it. I know I'd be angry and as I think this, I realize that lately I've been angry nearly every minute of every day. I've been angry with my mother, I suppose. Sure, her behavior embarrasses me. She's the town joke, after all. Actually, she's a tri-state joke. And probably, with this most recent arrest, her notoriety will spread even further and people across the entire Midwest will laugh at her. So yes, I am angry that my mother has embarrassed herself and by extension me.

It's more than anger, I realize, as I stand there looking back at Melody who continues to gaze at me with this nondescript look on her face. What I really feel is fear. Until a couple of months ago when all this started with her first arrest, my mother was, as far as I knew, perfectly sane and respectable. (Well, not *perfectly* sane. Who among us can make that claim?) But she was sane enough to get by in this world, the same way most of us do, one foot in front of the other, another day on the calendar, and our bills paid as best we can, our lives moving forward in some fashion. At some point though—and I realize with a jolt that I have no idea when—something happened and all her holding-it-together-ness disappeared, melted like a popsicle on an August afternoon. And I was left to deal with the sticky mess she left behind. Only, she hasn't gone anywhere. Have I asked my mother what changed in her life that made her think breaking into people's houses, etc., etc. was a viable idea? I haven't. In my anger, I have demanded to know what she could have been thinking when she did these things, but I never asked her what had changed in her life. I have never listened for an answer. All I've been thinking is that she's my mother and supposed to have the answers. I'm just her child, stumbling along while she's supposed to show me the way. Instead, I asked her questions that boiled down to how she could be doing this to *me*. Me. Always me.

I come back to myself and look up to see that Melody is still standing there, still watching. One part of my brain is formulating a plan for me to drive to my mother's house as soon as I can and speak to her as a caring human should. And simultaneously, another part of my brain is marveling over what I've just done, puzzling over why I've done it, and hoping to discover what I'm going to do next.

"I'm so sorry, Melody," I say.

She doesn't yell at me. If the situation was reversed, I'd be stomping and raging all over the place. I'd be so loud that anybody inside Carla's would come outside to check it out. What she does instead is, she smiles at me.

"I'll pay to get the tires fixed," I say. "Whatever it takes, don't worry. I'll pay for it." With a shock I realize she can probably see the Swiss Army knife in my hand. Does she think I shivved her tires?

"I'm not worried." She speaks calmly. She's more animated when she greets customers than she is right now.

"Look," I say, "Let's go inside and I'll call that tire guy in town and ask him to come over and fix all this. Or tow it to his shop. Whatever it takes." My eyes drift to the inside of Melody's car, and I notice something in the backseat. I look closer. There's a blanket folded there and next to it, a bed pillow. "I've got my credit card with me and..." I look closer still. There's a suitcase on the floor of the backseat. And on the seat itself there's a little plastic basket with toothpaste and a toothbrush and a curling iron and...

A thought hits my brain, or rather a sequence of thoughts: *Melody is sleeping in her car. Melody is living in her car. Melody is homeless.* Sure, something crazy is going on with my mother, and I'm embarrassed by it and sometimes people laugh at me because they know she's my mother, but so what? I can come back from that. I'm smart. I can figure out what's going on with her or how to get her help, and the problem can be addressed. But Melody has no place to go, and she's living in her car parked out behind Carla's Country Kitchen, a few feet from the dumpster where I toss congealed left-over Famous Mac and Cheese along with numerous other delights. She's homeless and that's awful.

No wonder Melody is always here, is always the first to arrive at Carla's, is always right there at the door waiting when I arrive to open the place. It's because she never goes home. And Melody's current address has three flat tires.

I stand there, Swiss army knife still in hand and think, *Kate, shame on you.* That's when I smile at Melody, and you know what? She smiles back. Not maliciously, like I would if our roles were reversed. But kindly. That is when I lose it, right then. That is precisely the moment my tears start.

Your Uncle Eddie

"We should call first," says Aunt Betsy. "People expect that nowadays."

"If they're family, they've no business being out on Sunday," my Uncle Eddie tells her. "Family should be right there at home, waiting to see who comes to visit."

We're doing the dinner dishes, my aunt and me. Uncle Eddie is standing in the kitchen behind us. Aunt Betsy has to keep turning halfway round just to talk to him.

"But it's different now," Aunt Betsy tries again. "A lot of people work on Sundays. Some people even go shopping. There are stores open on Sundays now. Not in East Liverpool, maybe, but in Youngstown. Somebody at bingo the other night was telling me about that."

"I never work on Sundays. Sunday is for family, and the stores got no business being open. There's six days a week to buy and sell and that's plenty."

Tonight, it's Aunt Betsy's turn to wash and I'm glad. She likes the water hot, hotter than I can stand. So tonight, I'm drying, which includes the putting away. I've been staying with my aunt and uncle for about two weeks now and I pretty well know where all the plates and spatulas go.

"Sunday is for family. Always was and always will be, so tomorrow we're gonna go visit Fritz and Jane."

My uncle walks over to the kitchen table. He moves the saltshaker so it's exactly next to the pepper, almost touching, like the shakers are a long-married couple. Then he goes out the door to see to the dog's dinner

95

*　　　*　　　*

Later that night my uncle comes into the living room where we're playing cards and says, "Hon, it's about time for Sheriff Matt Dillon. Bring me the chips and a beer, would ya?" He starts fiddling with the TV, and I go to the pantry and get out the big can of DanDee potato chips. I know this routine from last week. Aunt Betsy brings some cereal bowls, and Uncle Eddie dips one bowl at a time into the can. From where I'm sitting on the floor, I can hear the chips being scooped up, rustling like dried leaves. Pretty soon Uncle Eddie has three bowls with identical amounts of chips lined up on the coffee table. My aunt comes back from the kitchen. She's got a glass of beer for him and for us, two bottles of root beer. She hands me mine. It's cold, almost icy, and the bottle sweats in my hand. I can't help but think that if it had been my turn to wash those dishes it would almost be worth being in that hot, hot water to be able to hold this cold bottle afterwards.

Before Aunt Betsy sits down though, she stops halfway between my uncle and *Gunsmoke*. He looks at her, like he's waiting for something. And she looks right back and frowns. Then she sighs, goes back to the kitchen, and comes out with the salt shaker.

"Eddie, you know this is not good for you," she says in a voice that is sterner than when she yelled at me for accidentally letting the dog in the house. She hands him the shaker. "Do you want me to call that doctor right now and have him tell you again about this salt?"

"Hasn't hurt me yet," he says, and I'm thinking that this is the same conversation as last Saturday. My uncle shakes salt onto his bowl of chips, several good hard shakes, and then slowly sprinkles some into his beer. The beer foams up so much I can almost hear it, like it's an Alka-Seltzer for when you're sick. He holds it up as if he's waiting for the two of us to admire it, or maybe he's just admiring it himself. He looks as smug as a magician who's done a clever trick. But then the commercial ends, and Miss Kitty is in the Long Branch talking to Doc. And I know from last week that that there'll be no talking from now until the end of the show.

*　　　*　　　*

96

When I first came to stay with them, I was a little afraid of Uncle Eddie. Aunt Betsy had lived with me and my parents for a year back when I was in kindergarten, and she felt more like a big sister than an aunt. And since I didn't have any sisters (or brothers, for that matter), I liked that. But after she stayed with us for that year, she went home to Gram and sometime after that she met Uncle Eddie. I just never got to know him very well because it was always just the two of them going to the movies and the American Legion. So, I was happy to be asked to stay with them for a month that summer I was eleven while my mom was so sick. But before I left home my dad said something about Uncle Eddie's "peculiar eating habits." And I worried I might have to eat the sandwiches my dad said he made with pepperoni, a big slice of onion, and hot mustard. I didn't think I could eat those for a month. But Uncle Eddie only made one while I was there, and only asked me once if I'd like one too. When I said no thank you, he grinned at me with that chipped-tooth smile he had.

When I was at Gram's one time, she explained to me what she thought I needed to know about Uncle Eddie.

"The thing to remember about your Uncle Eddie," she said, "is that family is real important to him because he didn't have one when he was growing up. He was an orphan and didn't get adopted until this old couple took him in when he was twelve. The old man died a few month's later, but Lily, the woman, she was good to Eddie and finished raising him. After he left high school and got a job at the mill, he went out on his own. But no matter where he was, Eddie visited Lily every week—except for when he was in Korea, of course. Other than that, he'd spend a good part of every Sunday with her and that bug-eyed little dog she had. Now what kind of dog was that? Some kind of terrier, I think, though it looked like a rat. And what was that dog's name? I can't…oh, Stump. That was it. He was called Stump, but I don't know why. He had all his legs. Anyway, all the time Eddie was seeing your Aunt Betsy, he'd have Sunday dinner here with all of us, and then they'd drive over to Lily's where there'd be another meal waiting for them. This went on for years after they got married. You were old enough to remember that wedding, weren't you?"

No. I tried to remember it, but I couldn't. Not even when Aunt Betsy got their big wedding album down, all done up in white satin, and showed me all the pictures. And there I was with my mom and dad, wearing a pink dress and black patent leather Mary Janes. I can remember those shoes, remember how I'd pretend to be a tap dancer when I wore them, but not the wedding, though I must have been six or seven.

"A few years ago, Lily got sick and died, and Eddie was beside himself. He couldn't have mourned for that woman more if she were the mother who gave birth to him. She'd been poorly a long while before that, and so had Stump. Poor Eddie. His biggest worry for awhile there was which one was going to go first. It turned out Stump died first, but by then Lily was in the hospital and that damn doctor—excuse my language, honey—said he couldn't do any more for her which shook Eddie up, of course. He wouldn't tell Lily that Stump had died, said he just couldn't do it 'cause he didn't want to upset her. But before she got sick that last time, she made your Uncle Eddie swear that he'd bury Stump with her, right there in her coffin. He kept thinking she'd forget about that promise, I imagine, but just before she passed, she made him make that promise all over again, and even at the end, he wouldn't tell her that Stump had died some time ago. She wasn't in her right mind by then, I suppose, else she would have understood that she was putting Eddie in a pickle. What if Stump was still alive when she died? I told Eddie he should just tell her the truth cause the truth never hurt nobody, and it might even be a comfort to her knowing that Stump wasn't going to linger on without her. I mean, if Eddie was going to keep his promise, and if Stump hadn't already died, Eddie was going to have a time of it, deciding—well, never mind about that, honey. Eddie just kept saying Lily'd be so sad if she knew Stump died that it might kill her.

"And when Lily did die, it was a Friday morning, real early, sometime in August. I remember because the night before your

Uncle Fritz brought me a mess of fresh corn he'd picked and a bushel of those tomatoes, the big ones he knows I like. I had just gotten up and was thinking about the canning I'd have to do when Betsy called with the news. Well, then there was all that cooking we had to do to get ready for the funeral dinner—me and your mother and your Aunt Peg—and we were so busy I forgot all about Stump until Lily's funeral. The service was going to be at Dixon's Funeral Home—back when the old man still ran the place and not the son—after which we would all go to the grave and then come back here for the dinner. I'd told Red and Fritz, Squeak and Walt they'd have to take the day off and be there. The girls and I had already done all the work, so all the boys had to do was show up. 'Eddie doesn't have any family but us now,' I told them, 'and we need to stand right there by him.' And they listened. They could see I was serious.

"By the time I cleaned up the kitchen and got the neighbor to drive me into town for the service, there was your Uncle Eddie standing at the back of Dixon's front parlor, as far away from Lily's body as he could get. He was sweating into his good shirt and fidgeting, and I thought, 'oh, he is taking this hard, so hard.' But then he sidled up to me and said, 'I don't know how I'm gonna do it.' At first I thought he meant how was he gonna go on without Lily, but then he says, 'And *when* am I gonna do it?' Then I remembered about Stump and the promise he'd made. I was trying to think what to do when your Uncle Squeak came up and said he had it all figured out. He said Stump was out in the back of his truck, frozen. Turns out that when Stump died, Eddie had wrapped him up and froze him, put him in that big chest freezer he had in the garage—as far as I know he never did tell anybody where he kept Stump all that time, and I didn't care to hear any more about it. Anyway, Squeak had brought Stump with him to Dixon's, and 'All we need now,' Squeak says, 'is a distraction. Somebody's gotta get Dixon out of the way while the family is having its last quiet moment with the deceased.' And Squeak, who has always been a smart aleck, gave me that sly smile of his and says what they needed was for me to make a fuss at Theron Dixon about something, and act mean enough that he doesn't notice while some of the others get Stump where he needs to be.

"'What am I going to complain about?' I asked Squeak, and he winked and said he was sure I'd think of something. Well, when the time came we were all gathered together in the next room by the coffee, and Theron Dixon—he's a couple years older than me although we were the same class in school and what does that tell you about how smart he was?—I thought I could give him a hard time about the price of the service. With what he was charging for that coffin, he ought to be throwing the service in for free. At least I thought so, and I started to say so right there in view of the coffin, even raising my voice so he'd know I meant business, and he asked me would I be so kind as to speak with him in his office. And that, of course, was exactly what I wanted, to get him away from the coffin so the others could get Stump in there where Lily wanted him, so off I marched with him to his office.

"I was preparing to give him a piece of my mind for however long I thought the boys needed, but as soon as he shut the door, Theron says, 'Now, Elizabeth, are you really here to pick a fight about a funeral you're not paying for or is this about that dead dog thawing out in my parking lot?'

"Turns out that just before the service, Squeak and some of them had gone out back, hatching their plan and passing a flask around, acting like the fools they are and not noticing that Theron's son Buddy—they called him Buddy but he was really a junior—was right out there sneaking a cigarette and listening to every word.

"'Well, what are you going to do about this?' I asked Theron. 'The man promised the woman who loved him even more than the woman who birthed him that he'd—'

"'Why, Elizabeth, it's no business of mine what transacts between the griever and the grieved in these final moments of parting.' So, we sat down awhile, and talked about the old days at school and that time his daddy ran for county sheriff, and then I invited him and his boy to come over to the house for the funeral lunch. Seemed the decent thing to do, especially since he'd just offered to cut the price of the service in half without me having to badger him for long. Finally, we got up and joined the others at the coffin which was now shut. Nobody said anything. Eddie was looking at the rug again, and Squeak was redder in the face than usual. Theron Dixon reached into his pocket and came up with a little brass key that he put in the tiny brass lock on the coffin and turned it.

"'May Miss Lily rest in peace,' he said

"'And Stump too,' I said to myself before my little amen. And that was that. Now, I had always thought that Theron was a fool and the worst kind of fool at that, the kind that thinks he's better than other people, so I learned something that day. And your Uncle Eddie? I knew soon as Betsy first brought him home that he was a decent man, and I said so too. He loved Lily and visited her all those Sundays. And he saw to it that her last wish came true.'"

The credits to *Gunsmoke* haven't even started yet, and my Aunt Betsy says, "What about that time last year? It was a Sunday, remember? 'Let's go visit Squeak and Peg,' you said. 'No need to call. They're family,' you said. 'Here we go,' you said, so off we went.''

My aunt is talking to Uncle Eddie, but she is looking at me and smiling the whole time.

"Oh, we drive all the way over there, all the way over to the other side of Calcutta," my aunt says, "and have a terrible time getting up the lane cause it's muddy and rutted, but finally we make it, pull up by the house with mud splattered all over the car only to find that no one's home. And then you say that we're not waiting around. If they don't have the good sense to stay put on a Sunday, we're leaving, going right on back home, and then—"

"Oh, all right, all right," Uncle Eddie says, and I wonder if he is getting mad.

"—we drive all the way back home and what do we find? A note stuck in the back door from Squeak and it says: 'We were here and you weren't. Can't you folks ever just stay home on a Sunday?'"

My Aunt Betsy laughs and I do too after I look at Uncle Eddie to see if it's okay and it is.

"All right, Hon, I give up," Uncle Eddie says, and now he's laughing too. "You call them on Sunday and ask if they have plans. And if they're gonna be home, tell them to stay put."

LITTLE WORLDS

Phoebe dug through her purse. Her fingers located her billfold, a tube of hand lotion, a packet of tissues, and there, deep in a corner, her keys. She set the keys on the kitchen counter and stepped into the apartment's small bathroom to check her hair and makeup one more time. Back in the kitchen she took her last sips of morning coffee and reached into her purse for her keys. No keys. *Where could they be this time?* Phoebe sighed and tried again, fishing all the way to the purse's bottom and finally upending it onto the kitchen table. Amidst the rubble of grocery store coupons (*Probably expired but no time to check that now*), pennies, business cards and lip gloss was—of all things—her checkbook. Last night she'd spent twenty minutes searching her purse, her bedside table, the catchall drawer in the kitchen, and her car for her checkbook. She'd even called the Lots & Lots store where she'd stop for groceries after she left her job at the clinic. Her checkbook didn't seem to be there, she was told, and now, here it was, unearthed from her purse. *I did check my purse, didn't I?*

Two months ago, Phoebe had moved into a small apartment in her former hometown, and although she had only unpacked essentials, she had yet to gain control over her belongings. Haphazardly packed boxes still cluttered the hallway and a sizable chunk of the bedroom. She stared at the checkbook and wondered what it was she'd been thinking before she'd discovered it. *Oh yeah, the keys. Okay, relax. Everybody misplaces things from time to time. I, for example, have misplaced a husband—no, don't. You'll never get out of here if you start down that road. Focus, Phoebe. Find the keys so you can get to the workshop. That's the only thing you have to do right now. So when did I use them last? When I drove home from work yesterday? I drove home somehow, so where would I have put them when I got home?*

For the hundredth time Phoebe wondered why she couldn't pull herself together. Everything she did lately, every decision she made, seemed wrong, a series of mistakes that she might not be able to undo. She sighed. She gripped the kitchen table with both hands and took three deep breaths. *It's a new day, it's a new*—mid-mantra she spotted the keys on the kitchen counter.

The flyer said the workshop would begin at 9:00 a.m., so Phoebe had risen at 7:00, an hour earlier than she usually set the alarm on Saturdays. But here it was 8:50 and she was only just leaving the apartment. Was she lollygagging on purpose? Only yesterday she had been curious about the workshop's possibilities. While she was doing her laundry in the building's basement laundry room, shifting her bed sheets from washer to dryer, the bold headlines on the flyer caught her eye: "Are you SUDDENLY SINGLE?" She plunked coins in the dryer and walked over to the bulletin board for a closer look.

Are you SUDDENLY SINGLE?
Widowed? Divorced? Separated?
Join Melodi Clemens, author of *She Who Laughs Last Lasts*
for a morning of candor, wit, and joy—
Yes, JOY!

The grey-brown river nearly merged with the low-hung grey sky as Phoebe drove down the steep decline of St. Clair Avenue. Although it was only early October, winter seemed ready to descend. She turned into the Salvation Army parking lot, a two-story brick building dating back to the 1930s. Once inside, she found a handmade sign with the words "Singles Workshop"and an arrow pointing down the stairs. *People do get through this*, she said to herself, another of her mantras. When Brian first left, she had tried repeating "I can get through this" to herself over and over, but she was not sure that she personally could get through it. Better to phrase it generically: "people get through this." She could easily believe that some people do survive this sort of thing, but she didn't want to sap all the energy from her assertion with a qualification. No, "people get through this" captured just the right blend of hopefulness and realism. She would strive to follow the example of those people that she felt relatively certain did get through this. Her new heroes, these anonymous successes.

Downstairs, a redheaded woman, whom Phoebe sized up as about 30, stood at a podium and faced a roomful of folding chairs. The seating was about half full, she noted, and anemic sunlight trickled in from the room's high windows. At the rear of the room, an electric coffee urn gurgled. The room smelled of coffee and dust. A Salvation Army basement: just the place for disaster victims.

"Welcome! Come on in and have a seat." The redheaded woman smiled at Phoebe. "We haven't actually started yet." Phoebe winced an apology and forced herself to choose a seat near the front so she wouldn't be tempted to bolt for the door. Her only row mate was a young woman with chin-length hair who frowned and nodded when Phoebe mouthed a hello in her direction. As Phoebe got herself settled, she noticed that the back of the chair in front of her was stenciled with the words "Marting Funeral Home," a detail that made her think of deckchairs on the Titanic. *Gotta remember to tell Brian about that… oh, never mind.* Like a squirrel gathering acorns, she had the habit common to the married of storing up small observations to share with her spouse over dinner.

"—so here she is! Melodi! Clemens!" The redheaded woman extended her arm as if a velvet curtain were about to part so a spotlight could shine on the star of the show. Phoebe stifled a giggle and used this pause, for applause presumably, as an opportunity to steal a glance back at her fellow Suddenly Singles. One hundred percent of them were female, she noted, with at least a third looking stricken, another third appearing maniacally chipper, and the final third giving every appearance of being thoroughly angry. *Maybe it should be called the Sullenly Singles.* Phoebe suddenly longed for a group of women friends who would call themselves such a thing. The Sullenly Singles, women who would meet once a week to complain about the small, daily catastrophes of their lives, celebrate their successes, sample each other's appetizers, and tell outrageously dirty jokes. And then, and only if necessary, weep.

But now, here in front of her was Melodi Clemens herself, famed authoress and star of workshop flyers in apartment laundry rooms. Wearing a well-tailored black pantsuit and a chunky silver necklace, she had a pixie cut of blonde hair and a model's high cheekbones. Melodi Clemens was impressively put together.

"So, tell me," Melodi Clemens began as if they were old friends. "Have you ever broken down and sobbed in, say, the misses department at Macy's? Have you left your house only later to discover that the shirt you were wearing was inside out? Have you found yourself watching infomercials at 4:00 a.m. and suddenly Magic Microwave Grillers and Miracle Steam Cleaners appear on your doorstep? Do you avoid mirrors, not because your new life is aging you—your bones tell you it's aging you—but because the person looking back at you doesn't look even the least bit familiar?"

Melodi paused, scanned the room, and then laughed. "Well, that was me. Oh my gosh, all that and so much more! I don't want to tell you how many times I ran out of gas because I wasn't paying attention, or about the time I decided to treat myself to dinner at Pittsburgh's finest restaurant only to discover halfway through the entree that I'd forgotten my purse." Melodi Clemens laughed again. Apparently, she could find this disfunction amusing, now that she was safe on the other shore.

"Oh, I was a Grade A mess! I was a crazy person for more than a year, maybe two full years, barely able to move myself from point A to point B."

Oh, good news, Phoebe thought. *I can look forward to being screwed up for a couple of years, then? Delightful.*

"And here is the good news," Melodi Clemens' eyes swept the room and stopped at Phoebe's.

Did I say that out loud?

Then, as if she were gossiping in church, Melodi Clemens lowered her voice to nearly a whisper. "I want you to know, ladies, that I have been through it all and lived to tell about it.

"And I didn't just survive the experience," Melodi continued. "In fact, I found ways in spite of—or perhaps because of— my experience to get myself on the right track for the first time in my life. It might be hard to believe, but I did become a stronger, more confident and yes, happier woman."

It sounded like fire walking to Phoebe, this idea of passing through some ordeal and emerging, altered and improved, someplace else. Or a fantasy novel where the hero crosses into a new world as easily as stepping through a magical arch.

Melodi Clemens launched into her story: the decades-long marriage, "the fabulous house," the pride she had taken in the chain of pizza shops she and her husband successfully managed. Her certainty that all was well in her life until the day she opened the back door of one of their restaurants and found her husband in what she delicately called "an unseemly embrace" with their newest hire, an eighteen-year-old waitress. The rapid crumbling of her household after that. The night her husband stomped out, then returned in a rage when his girlfriend's parents wouldn't let him move into their house with her. And then the long weeks that followed, as she repeatedly demeaned herself with teary phone calls in which she begged him for an explanation and a second chance.

"Some of that is a blur, and for that I am profoundly grateful," Melodi Clemens said. "But I do remember howling. Howling like an abandoned dog."

Was howling in Phoebe's future? *Wonderful.*

It was the howling that did it. Phoebe suddenly remembered one particular night a couple of days after Brian left. She had fallen in her living room, tripping over nothing other than her own feet, and stayed there, face down on the floor, the carpet scratchy against her cheek, wondering how to get up. Wondering *why* to get up. Eventually, she got on all fours and prepared to stand when her chest constricted, and she started coughing. The coughing led to gasping which led to gagging. There had not been any howling, but there was such primal pain and panic. And fear, fear that nothing in her life would ever be okay ever again. She finally stood up, but the realization that the one person she would have turned to for comfort from that pain had shut himself off from her almost put her back on the floor. Thinking of it now, with Melodi Clemens a few feet in front of her and speaking so casually of her past life, Phoebe felt the same chest-tightening panic. She had to get out.

Phoebe stood up and stumbled out of her row, doing her best to keep her head down so as not to see Melodi Clemens' reaction to her departure. She could feel Melodi's eyes on her, but she kept moving, heading towards the door. She was stopped by the redheaded woman.

"You're not leaving, I hope," the redheaded woman said in a stage whisper. "She's just about to get to the good part."

"Oh, sorry, I just remembered that I have to—"

"It would be a shame if you were to miss the best part."

"Yes, but I—"

"Well, please take this with you and consider signing up for Melodi's workshop series. It could change your life, you know." They were in the hall now, the woman having followed her out the door. She held out a brochure and smiled at her. "There's only so much Melodi can do in this short presentation, but the workshop series, well, it's life changing. It changed mine. It really is worth the money."

"Thanks for the flyer, but I don't think—"

"Of course, you have to want to have your life changed."

"Oh, but—"

"How about Melodi's book then? There are only a few copies left. It keeps selling out, you know. Would you like to buy a copy before you go?"

"No, thanks, not just now, no."

"It's all there on the brochure—how to order the book or enroll in the series," the redheaded woman said as Phoebe started up the basement steps. "It's all there."

*   *   *

In the Salvation Army parking lot, Phoebe took three deep breaths. *People get through this, people get through this, people get through this.* The day seemed sunnier now, and yes, it was definitely warming up. Maybe Autumn wasn't going to speed by so quickly after all. She glanced at the brochure. Melodi Clemens was offering an eight-week workshop series for $350. Registration was limited, so she should act now, the text admonished. All major credit cards were accepted.

Nope. No. Definitely not. Not doing that.

Once she was in her car, Phoebe hesitated before starting the engine. She had no desire to go back to the apartment. It wasn't home. That seemed odd because she had grown up in East Liverpool. True, she'd lived for the last twelve years in Cleveland, but her first twenty years had been spent right here. Her parents had moved to Florida the year after her marriage and died there only a year apart shortly thereafter. She had no other family, and she'd lost touch with her high school friends. Still, when she thought about what she might do when it was clear her marriage was ending, where she might go, this was the only place that came to mind.

When Brian left, calling her from his job one day to tell her he was through, she panicked. She forced herself into work the next day, determined to behave as if this event hadn't happened, but as soon as she saw Deb, the receptionist in her department, she had, in a gush of tears and snot, told her everything. Deb dragged her to the women's room, washed her face off as if she were a hysterical child, drove her home, and put her to bed. Only later did Phoebe find out that Deb had driven back to work and said to their co-workers, "You'll never guess! Phoebe's husband has left her."

Between that shame and living in the empty house, Phoebe felt the urge to get out as quickly as possible. She cut all ties in Cleveland, amazed at how easy it had been. A few internet searches and one drive to East Liverpool got her an apartment. And finding a new job had been even easier. She was an MRI tech and fortunately, a health center in East Liverpool had an opening. It all worked out so smoothly, and only four weeks after Brian left, Phoebe was heading south again, this time for a permanent move back to a place where she might nestle in, and then slowly, when she was ready, unfurl, like the ferns in the rock garden she was leaving behind in Cleveland.

Still, Phoebe sat in her car in the parking lot. She wondered if she had abandoned her former life too quickly. Had she been in any condition to make such a quick decision? Was this a healthy new start? Or was she running away from her problems? She had been so focused on updating her resume and packing that she hadn't reflected on what she was doing until it was already done.

Fortunately, she liked her work, both at the hospital in Cleveland and her new position in East Liverpool. Her work had provided the distraction that got her through the last couple of months. And she was good at her job. Her special skill was spotting claustrophobes. Patients didn't always know that about themselves, as she had quickly learned when she was new on the job. Not only could Phoebe identify them, she could talk them down, ease them onto the MRI's table, and coach and coax them to completion. And after the scan, she could remain friendly and helpful without betraying any may-God-help-you thoughts if she saw some anomaly, some looming catastrophe, on the control room monitor. The MRI might be a revealer of secrets, but it wasn't her place to burst out with the news, good, bad, or otherwise.

Her training had provided her an understanding of the science behind the MRI and an appreciation of its ability to make the unseen visible, exposing calamities of the body. Her training had, in fact, provided her with some firsthand knowledge when the instructor had urged students to experience the MRI for themselves, to climb onto the table and enter that world.

"Who wants to go first?" The instructor raised her eyebrows at the students clustered nearest to the MRI. "I want you to know a little something of what patients experience, and the only way to do that is to climb aboard and try it out." She patted the table as if it were a pony and whoever volunteered first was about to go for a gentle ride around the paddock.

Phoebe's was the only hand that went up. She stretched out on the table, and after a few words of encouragement from her instructor, was pulled into the tube as if she were a sausage sliding into its casing. Phoebe was aware of the smoothness of the tube's sides and its overwhelming whiteness enveloping her. She closed her eyes.

"Okay in there, Phoebe?" Her instructor's voice came at her over a loudspeaker in the tube. "I'm going to give you a few minutes in there, okay?"

"Fine, yes, I'm fine." Phoebe replied. *Breathe. Breathe deep.*

Tap Tap Tap Tap Tap Tap Tap

Bang Bang Bang Bang Bang

From pianissimo to fortissimo and back again, the MRI clanked and clattered. At one point, Phoebe imagined monstrous night insects engaged in some primordial call and response. The shudder of thuds and thumps gave way to a steady drone of pulsating buzzes, and soon—too soon—the instructor's voice came over the speaker again, asking if she were still doing fine. And then out she slid, deposited once again into the outer world where the instructor beamed down at her.

"Okay, then Phoebe? Not so bad, was it?"

"No, no, it was fine," Phoebe said. She wanted to say more, wanted to say that she had, in fact, enjoyed it, but the grim expressions on her classmates' faces suggested that was not going to be the majority view, so she simply smiled.

Phoebe drove past her apartment complex. She slowed as she neared the Lots & Lots store. *Do I need anything? Should I stop? No, no point going in there and roaming.* She kept going. Just beyond the store's massive parking lot was a small shopping strip she hadn't noticed before. The most prominent sign for the stores there was for a florist.

Flowers. Phoebe had once read in a woman's magazine that buying yourself a bouquet of fresh flowers was a simple way to lift your spirits. Self care, the author had called it. "Treat yourself like you would a dear friend." Phoebe would do just that: buy herself a bouquet of flowers and then head back to the apartment. Flowers would certainly cost less than Melodi Clemens' book or workshops. But as Phoebe reached for the shop door, the sun emerged from behind a cloud, and a shaft of light blinded her. She fumbled for the door handle and stepped inside the business only to realize that she was not in a florist's shop at all. This was, judging from the shelves of dog food in front of her, a pet store. Had she grabbed the wrong handle? Had she ended up in the business next to the florist?

"Hi, I'll be right with you," called out a female voice. Phoebe looked around, but she didn't see a clerk. The only customer, a woman in her sixties, stood in front of a large birdcage populated by a dozen or so jittering parakeets. The woman made kissy sounds at them. "Pretty, pretty," she said. Phoebe remembered that her grandmother had always had a parakeet. She had lived in a one-bedroom trailer, where the bird cage dominated a corner of her tiny dining area. Every time someone bumped into the cage, the bird muttered dark objections. Over the years there had been a sequence of parakeets, in various colors, and all named Pretty Boy. On one visit to her grandmother, Pretty might be the most beautiful shade of blue, but on her next visit, where blue Pretty had been, a green parakeet now huddled in the cage. When she was a child, Phoebe had been convinced that her grandmother owned a single magical bird who could change his color at will. Now though, she wondered if someone had told her this so she wouldn't ask what had happened to the previous Pretty Boy.

"Ok, now what can I help you with?" Phoebe had been looking over a rack of bright dog collars and leashes, an interesting array of patterns and colors including peace signs, daisies, and Day of the Dead skulls. She turned now and saw a teenage girl before her, seventeen maybe, with short brown hair and an impossibly bright orange tee shirt with her faded jeans.

"Oh, I don't know. I'm new here and I thought…" *Thought what, exactly?* "Well, I wondered if I might like to get a pet of some sort."

"Oh, okay," smiled the girl. "What did you have in mind? We don't sell puppies or kittens ourselves, but we usually have some cats from the animal shelter. You know, ones they adopt out. They didn't bring us any this week, so—"

"No, I just moved into an apartment. Something lower maintenance, I guess."

"We specialize in tropical fish. There's a whole room back here just full of them. Would you be interested in a tank of fish? They're pretty low key. You can't take them for a walk or anything," and here she laughed, "but they are restful. Calming, you know. That's why there used to be so many aquariums in doctor's offices."

Phoebe suddenly remembered that the dentist she went to as a child had an aquarium on the wall of his waiting area.

"Oh, I never thought of that. Makes sense, I guess. Well, is it complicated? Where do I start? I mean, if I wanted to get one, how would I start?"

"It's pretty easy. You have to set up the tank first and let it sit for a few days with the water in it and the filter running before you introduce any fish. And then you have to acclimate the fish to the tank so they don't have any sudden shocks. They have to adjust to their new environment, you see. All that means is that you let the plastic bag with the fish in it float in the tank for awhile and then gradually...."

Phoebe must have looked confused because the girl was quick to add "Look, it's not really as complicated as I'm making it sound. It's all about helping them adjust to the change, see?"

"Sure, I understand."

As they talked the girl led her to the back room which was indeed full of fish tanks, long and high shelves lined with them, a couple dozen at least, all gurgling away. The room glowed with the lights on each tank creating the sensation of a room full of tiny distinct worlds.

"We've got all kinds of fish, as you can see."

Phoebe bent to peer into a tank with a couple dozen small, torpedo-shaped fish, each adorned with a streak of electric blue and a smear of scarlet.

"Those are one of my favorites—neon tetras." The girl smiled. "You can see how they got their name." Phoebe noticed that the fish flashed their bright colors as they swam. "They are a little delicate, so you shouldn't take any of those home until the tank is well established, mature as they call it. And you need a bunch of them—fifteen or twenty or more cause they're what's called a shoaling fish. They need each other to survive."

Phoebe looked up. "Is that like a school of fish?"

"Not exactly. Schooling fish swim in formation, as if someone had choreographed their moves. You know, they turn in unison and stuff. Shoaling fish are a little more independent. They don't swim in group formations exactly, but they need to be around each other. They sort of hang out together, if you see what I mean."

Phoebe nodded, realizing that she was in the presence of someone who really enjoyed what she was doing, someone who knew what she was talking about. She remembered what a delight that was to talk with someone who was enthusiastic about her job. Such enthusiasm might be contagious.

She had meant to politely, gratefully, thank the clerk and leave. She meant to drive back to her apartment, meant to start a pot of chicken noodle soup and a load of laundry. Then, after she'd performed those tasks, she would sit and carefully consider whether she really wanted an aquarium or not.

But that was what she usually did—took her time pondering a decision. *I thought long and hard before marrying Brian and look how that turned out.* She usually thought about decisions for so long that she invariably moved from careful consideration to agony, weighing all the pros and cons over and over until a rational decision became impossible. It was only recently that she made quick decisions—like quitting her job and leaving Cleveland, opting for the first apartment she looked at, agreeing to take the first job she was offered.

Was all this quick decision making instinct or foolishness? She'd find out soon enough. And if it all had been a mistake, she'd find some way to redirect herself to something better. In the meantime, though, what was one more fast decision?

So, Phoebe nodded as the girl talked her through all the equipment she'd need—the filter and heater and gravel and thermometer and the tank itself. She kept nodding as her various choices piled up on the counter. Once she'd selected the plastic figure of a little deep sea diver and a miniature treasure chest that appeared chockfull of gold coins and goblets, she felt certain that following this impulse was the right thing to do.

"When you come for the fish, we'll talk about which ones live compatibly with which," the girl advised. "You gotta be careful though," she added as she carried the tank and all its equipment out to Phoebe's car. "Once you get one tank underway, you start thinking about the next one. And so on. That's how my dad and I got started. And he said that once you end up with a roomful of fish tanks you may as well open a pet store."

Phoebe left the store beaming, the proud owner of a little world-to-be that she alone would be in charge of. Already she could imagine herself rolling up her sleeve and reaching into the tank to adjust a plant or the deep sea diver, reaching down like the hand of God while tetras flashed and darted just beyond her reach.

Sorry Excuse

Every time Mama gets on the phone to call into the QVC, the kids whirl around the living room like tops. Like tops gone crazy. Like tops that got batteries like that bunny on TV. She shushes them and waves them back away from her the whole time she's on the phone, but they keep spinning and whirling, whispering and giggling. She puts her finger in one ear while she tries to confirm her address and tell them she wants the shoes in taupe and black and what they call True Navy. The kids keep dancing all over like it's Christmas morning. I can't figure what those kids are thinking.

It's not like Santa himself is gonna show up at the door with toys and baby dolls. All that happens is, after a few days the UPS guy pulls up. I hear the truck before I see it—it sounds throatier than the postman's little sawed-off jeep—and then he backs into the drive like he's planning on a fast getaway. I can hear him run up the steps, knock on the door, and drop the boxes on the porch. If the blinds are up and if I slide my eyes to the right just so, I can see him, a blur of brown uniform. The boxes thud when he drops them, and then I hear the truck pull out and gripe a little when he shifts into second. And you know what? Those kids go wild all over again. Like it's the Easter bunny or somebody come to take them to the circus.

"It's the ups man," the kids scream. They always call him that, the ups man, and I want to tell them it's U-P-S which stands for...I forget what. But they are wound up, wound up tight, and they scramble over each other to get the door open, like puppies tumbling down the stairs, each one trying to get to the boxes and bring them in the house. And then they're all shouting for Mama who is usually lying down at that time of day, taking her rest.

"You got boxes," they shout, and Mama comes out from the bedroom, smoothing her housecoat and twisting her neck that's always troubling her with aches. She sits in the fuzzy green chair, her favorite, even though the arms are worn bare and the cushion droops in the middle like a sad smile. And she sighs.

"You open them up," she says, meaning the kids, not me. "Mama's too tired."

So, the kids tear into those boxes as if there's treasure inside, squabbling over who gets to open what, and when they do get them open they gasp over the shoes like they've never seen such beauty. Then they get quiet and lay the shoes out on the rug in front of Mama's chair, petting them like there were everybody's favorite newborn babies. And then everybody stares at them like they might get up and do a trick.

"Look Mama," they say. "Shoes for you."

"Oh yeah," she says. "I forgot about those."

Mama groans as she bends over to pick up the shoes. She scoops them up in her big arms all at once, hugs them as if they were a pile of warm towels. She leans her head back so she can see them all, looks them over like she's counting their toes, and sighs again.

"I thought the jewelry would be here by now," she says and frowns. "You kids take these boxes away." And the kids fight over the shoe boxes. The littler ones come away with only a lid. The least one ends up with nothing and starts in crying.

"Take those boxes and get out of here," Mama says. "Go on back to your room." And they are off, tromping down the basement steps. Mama takes her shoes with her back to her bedroom, and then it's just me here in the living room. I want to ask is someone gonna start dinner. The noise of the kids gets softer once they get to the basement. Pretty soon I hear Mama's bed creak as she lays herself back down, and the house is quiet again, and I got some time to try to think about things. Things like how did I, Walter Meadows, get here and what's wrong that my legs don't work. But the sun is warming my back, and I can feel myself ready to nod off again. I feel puny as a pup most of the time, so when Mama gives me my medicine I just nod right off.

Next thing I know, somebody is rapping at the door. They knock and then they knock some more, but no one comes. There's no sound from the basement. Mama musta had them take their medicine too. Nothing from the bedroom either, except Mama's breathing deep, like a bear in its den. I slide my eyes toward the front door. All I can see is a little head with tiny, tiny grey curls on it.

Then I see these bright eyes looking through the window. It's a woman. She's got her hand across her forehead so she can squint in, her eyes shiny, darting. Can she see me? I can see her good now, see a cross on a silver chain round her neck, see that her eyes are blue, that watery blue like Helen's were, but I don't know if she can see me.

"Well, hello there," the tiny woman says. "Could someone come to the door?" She is loud but little, a short woman rapping hard on the window now. It's the witch! The woman from next door that Mama and the kids talk about. From the bedroom I can hear Mama rustling.

"Are you okay in there? Are you alone?" the witch says, looking right at me. She smiles.

"Just a minute, I'm coming," Mama says, moving fast to the door. She opens it a crack.

"Oh, hello. I'm your neighbor Agnes, but you can call me Aggie. I'm in the blue house right next door. Been meaning to come over for a couple weeks to welcome you to the neighborhood, but I thought I ought to let you get settled in first. Mind if I come in for a minute?"

Before Mama gets her mouth open, the witch is in the door. She is inside the house. She looks from Mama to me and back to Mama, smiling the whole time. She's wearing some kind of dark skirt and blue shirt and man boots, and looks even littler than she did outside. Mama smiles back at her and looks about to say something.

"It's just that I have an excuse to come over now 'cause we're having a little neighborhood Halloween party this Saturday at noon. It's always at my house 'cause I don't have dogs. I couldn't help but notice you have some children here, and you are all invited. We got lots of kids on this street. I bet they'd love to meet your family."

She does put me in mind of a witch now that I see her full on, except for her nose. Her nose is too small for a witch. This is the first time I've laid eyes on her, but the kids talk about her all the time. "Ding dong, ding dong," they sing. "Witch, witch, witch."

"I'm not sure we'll be home on Saturday."

"Bring your father too," the witch says, and I want to tell her that Mama's not my daughter. Some sort of niece is what she is, but as many times as Mama has explained, I can't figure it. I only had the one brother, Vernon, and no sisters, and Vernon never married, so I don't know how exactly Mama and I are kin. "The daughter of your second cousin is a niece," Mama keeps telling me, but I don't see it. "That just shows you're getting old," she always says.

"What's your name?" The witch asks me, leaning in toward me a little. The silver cross on a chain at her neck swings in my direction.

I want to tell her, but Mama says, "Oh, this is my Uncle Pete."

The witch keeps her eyes on me. "Can he hear me?" she asks Mama while she's still looking at me, and I want to say "Hell yes, I can hear you. I can hear what those kids are up to in the basement right now too, probably messing with my tools again." But no, that can't be right. I don't think this is my house. I don't think my tools are down there.

"No," Mama says. "The poor thing has gone deaf from all those years in the steel mill, and he's shy to boot."

"I never worked in the mill a day in my life," I want to say. The potteries is where I worked. It's where a lot of us worked back then, even the women. Less money than the mills but safer, no chance of winding up in an ingot. I can't stop looking at the witch who is still

119

looking me over. She's not young, I can see from all the grey hair, and while she's this close I can see wrinkles around her eyes and mouth. Laugh lines, Helen called them. "If only I hadn't lived a life, hadn't laughed and cried, I wouldn't be so wrinkled now," she would say.

"He has his ways," Mama says. "You know how these old ones are." And when she says "old ones" the witch twitches a little. Not her whole body, just her right eye, like she's got a little tic. She blinks a few times and smiles at me some more.

"Does he talk?"

I want to say, "Of course. I can talk. What do you wanna talk about?"

"He talks to us is all. Like I said, he's shy." Mama has that edge to her voice now, the one that comes just before she starts in shouting at those kids.

"I'm so sorry, I didn't catch your name" the woman says, smiling at Mama. There is a lot of smiling going on here, but I can see there are two kinds—the icy ones and the warm ones.

"I'm Dawn," says Mama. I'm not sure I knew that.

"How old is Uncle Pete?" the woman asks, and Mama looks like she's thinking. I start thinking too. How old am I? How old would Vernon be if he'd lived? Maybe Mama's got me mixed up with Vernon. But how could that be? He died in the mill a long time ago. Not even thirty years old. A terrible thing, they all said, and the company gave us a steel ingot weighed about as much as Vernon so we'd have something to bury. That happened sometimes in those days. No body. Now here I sit and all I am is body, not that this body is much good to me.

"Oh, he's funny about that. Too vain to tell us his real age, you know. Just keeps saying he's thirty-nine. But he's got to be, oh, what do you think, Uncle Pete?" And Mama looks at me as if I might say something. "You must be in your eighties by now, right?"

"Oh, I almost forgot," the woman says. "The mailman brought me something by mistake this morning that I thought might be yours. But the name on it isn't Pete. Isn't Dawn neither." She pulls an envelope out of a pocket in her long skirt. Mama

120

reaches her hand out, like she will take that envelope, but the woman isn't offering it. She just looks at it and says, "Says here it's from the government of the United States so it must be important."

Mama strains her neck, trying to get a good look at the envelope. She'll be complaining about that neck later on, all through *Jeopardy*.

"Is it from the IRS? They do plague people, don't they?" Mama gives a little laugh.

"Well, let me look," says the woman, and she pulls the envelope in closer to herself and squints at it. Then she pulls it even closer, practically onto her little nose. It's almost as funny as that silly stuff Red Skelton did on TV. Helen and I watched his show every week, and we laughed and laughed.

"Why no, it's from the Social Security Administration." In a flash, Mama grabs at the envelope, but the woman is quick and turns her body so Mama can't reach it.

"But this says it's for a Walter Meadows, so there must be some mistake. No, this is all wrong. It's your address, but it must not be for your Uncle Pete." Her eye is quivering again.

"Walter is Uncle Pete's first name," Mama says, and she and the woman stare at each other.

Something is happening.

The two women just stand there, still as snowmen, still staring at each other. Neither is flashing any kind of a smile. This goes on for so long that I wonder if they will do it for the rest of the day. If I had a camera, I would take a picture of this so I could study it later. Then I could say, "Yes, this is it, the exact second just before the first punch was thrown." The only thing I'm wondering now is, who is gonna to make the first move?

The little woman's eye is twitching fast, like it's sending out signals in secret code.

Mama holds out her hand, waiting for the woman to put the envelope in it, I guess, and the woman does so, but slowly, slowly, while she's got both the quiet eye and the blinky eye on Mama the whole time.

Something is happening here.

"Well, I'm glad I brought it over to you," says the woman with a smile, one of the icy kind. "I'll just be on my way then." She starts for the door but stops and turns back to me. She leans down and places her hand on mine. Her hand is cool and soft. "So nice to meet you, Mr. Meadows," she says and smiles one of the warm ones into my eyes. "I'll be seeing you again soon."

"Jesus God," says Mama when the woman is gone. "Good riddance." She's on her way to the kitchen, to start dinner maybe. Then I hear her yelling down the stairs for those kids to come back up.

"I'll be seeing you again soon" is what the tiny woman said to me. I wonder if her ticky eye was sending me some other message too.

Something was happening, and what it was, what I didn't know for a long time, was that Aggie got the authorities involved. I don't remember going to the hospital, but that's where I landed. The doctors there discovered that Mama had doped me up with amphetamines and sleeping pills and who knows what all and that I was dehydrated. They also figured out that my legs and brain work just fine. Meanwhile, back at Mama's, there were cops and social workers running all around the place. Mama was hauled off one way, and the kids were hauled off the other way. Guess they had a time of it, sorting out who all those kids belonged to and how Mama got hold of them. Turns out none of them were hers. Not a one.

I felt bad about it all, especially about the kids, but Aggie said, "Don't. Don't you dare feel bad. That woman took advantage of you and wasn't much better to those kids. That so-called Mama pretended to be your family and kidnapped you and stole your money, so don't you waste a tear on the likes of her. She wouldn't cry for you any."

Couple days later Aggie and me got our picture in the paper. She brought it to me while I was still in the hospital. The reporter called Aggie an angel, "an angel in our midst" which made her laugh out loud. "Oh boy, if only my mother were alive to hear that," she said. "She never thought I was angel material, that's for sure."

The reporter overdid it, if you ask me. He went on and on about Aggie, "diminutive Aggie," he called her, and "not your average grandmotherly type." She did not like that diminutive stuff. "Makes me sound like some kind of midget, but I don't think you're supposed to call them that anymore."

The only thing that really riled Aggie was that Mama didn't get marched out of her house in handcuffs when they came for her. "They let her walk out under her own steam, held the door of the police car open for her nice as you please, and treated her like a queen," Aggie said. "She's no queen and she was nobody's mama."

When we went to court for the sentencing, the judge called Mama "a sorry excuse for a human being," so now Aggie and me refer to her that way. It's as good a name for her as any. I thought we were gonna get tossed right out of the courtroom when the judge said that because Aggie took to laughing so hard. She settled right down though when the judge shot her a hard look. Mama refused to apologize to me like the judge wanted her to, and after that it was all over. Aggie and me went back to her place.

"Breaded pork chops," she said, "with sauerkraut, green beans, and applesauce. How's that sound for tonight's dinner?"

"Sounds delicious," I said. She started to open the fridge but turned back to me and smiled.

"Walter, do you know who Pretty Boy Floyd was?"

"Sure. Bank robber. Got himself killed by the FBI not far from here. Why?"

"No reason."

Later on, while I was sitting at the kitchen table smelling all that good food being prepared by a good woman, I gazed out the window and over at Mama's place and thought how lucky I am. I have never been what you might call sought after by women, not even when I was young and not so bad to look at. Now look at me.

If my brother Vernon were here, he'd have something to say about the fact that not one but two women got hold of me and moved me into their homes. Oh, he'd get a kick out of that all right.

I get quite a kick out of it myself.

ABOUT THE AUTHOR

Karen Kotrba was raised in Columbiana County, Ohio and taught composition at Baldwin-Wallace University, Youngstown State University, and Kent State University in East Liverpool. A graduate of the Northeast Ohio MFA program, she is the recipient of an Ohio Arts Council grant for individual excellence in fiction writing. Her poetic sequence about the midwives of the Frontier Nursing Service, *She Who is Like a Mare*, was also published by Bottom Dog Press.

BOOKS BY BOTTOM DOG PRESS

APPALACHIAN WRITING SERIES

Pottery Town Blues, Karen Kotrba, 128 pgs, $16
Labor Days, Labor Nights: More Stories, Larry D. Thacker, 208 pgs, $18
The Long Way Home, Ron Lands, 170 pgs, $18
Mingo Town & Memories, Larry Smith, $15
40 Patchtown: A Novel, Damian Dressick, 184 pgs, $18
Mama's Song, P. Shaun Neal, 238 pgs, $18
Fissures and Other Stories, by Timothy Dodd, 152 pgs, $18
Old Brown, by Craig Paulenich, 92 pgs, $16
A Wounded Snake: A Novel, by Joseph G. Anthony, 262 pgs, $18
Brown Bottle: A Novel, by Sheldon Lee Compton, 162 pgs, $18
A Small Room with Trouble on My Mind, by Michael Henson, 164 pgs, $18
Drone String: Poems, by Sherry Cook Stanforth, 92 pgs, $16
Voices from the Appalachian Coalfields, by Mike and Ruth Yarrow,
Photos by Douglas Yarrow, 152 pgs, $17
Wanted: Good Family, by Joseph G. Anthony, 212 pgs, $18
Sky Under the Roof: Poems, by Hilda Downer, 126 pgs, $16
Green-Silver and Silent: Poems, by Marc Harshman, 90 pgs, $16
The Homegoing: A Novel, by Michael Olin-Hitt, 180 pgs, $18
She Who Is Like a Mare: Poems of Mary Breckinridge and the Frontier Nursing Service,
by Karen Kotrba, 96 pgs, $16
Smoke: Poems, by Jeanne Bryner, 96 pgs, $16
Broken Collar: A Novel, by Ron Mitchell, 234 pgs, $18
The Pattern Maker's Daughter: Poems, by Sandee Gertz Umbach, 90 pgs, $16
The Free Farm: A Novel, by Larry Smith, 306 pgs, $18
Sinners of Sanction County: Stories, by Charles Dodd White, 160 pgs, $17
Learning How: Stories, Yarns & Tales, by Richard Hague, $18
The Long River Home: A Novel, by Larry Smith,
230 pgs, cloth $22; paper $16

APPALACHIAN WRITING SERIES ANTHOLOGIES

Unbroken Circle: Stories of Cultural Diversity in the South,
Eds. Julia Watts and Larry Smith, 194 pgs, $18
Appalachia Now: Short Stories of Contemporary Appalachia,
Eds. Charles Dodd White and Larry Smith, 178 pgs, $18
Degrees of Elevation: Short Stories of Contemporary Appalachia,
Eds. Charles Dodd White and Page Seay, 186 pgs, $18
Free Shipping.
http://smithdocs.net

BOOKS BY BOTTOM DOG PRESS

HARMONY SERIES

Bottom Dog Press, Inc.
P.O. Box 425 /Huron, Ohio 44839
http://smithdocs.net